The Tiger Bone Thief

RICHARD KIDD

Illustrated by Peter Bailey

CORGI YEARLING BOOKS

With thanks to ... ... n the art
of taxiderm... ... ... n Zoo

THE TIGER BONE THIEF
A CORGI YEARLING BOOK : 0 440 864526

First publication in Great Britain

PRINTING HISTORY
Corgi Yearling edition published 2002

1 3 5 7 9 10 8 6 4 2

Set in 12/15pt Palatino by
Falcon Oast Graphic Art Ltd

Corgi Yearling Books are published by Transworld Publishers,
61–63 Uxbridge Road, London W5 5SA,
a division of The Random House Group Ltd,
in Australia by Random House Australia (Pty) Ltd,
20 Alfred Street, Milsons Point, Sydney, NSW 2061, Australia,
in New Zealand by Random House New Zealand Ltd,
18 Poland Road, Glenfield, Auckland 10, New Zealand
and in South Africa by Random House (Pty) Ltd,
Endulini, 5a Jubilee Road, Parktown 2193, South Africa.

Made and printed in Great Britain by
Clays Ltd, St Ives plc.

1

The Frightened Eye

I found it late one Friday afternoon, at the beginning of autumn, when I was coming home from school. It was lying face down on the muddy path that follows the stream alongside the Old Manor House. It was a chance in a million, a real needle in a haystack. The thing was, it looked exactly like a dead oak leaf and there were plenty of them, millions, all mixed with willow leaves and apple leaves in a thick, soggy carpet of yellows and browns.

But I didn't miss it; against all the odds it stood out. Maybe it was its flatness, or the way the light fell on it, but something caught my eye. I stopped and picked it up, exploring its irregular, rounded edges with my finger and thumb. One side was plain cardboard and the other side, the picture side, was covered in mud so I wiped it clean on the sleeve of my jacket and when I held it up close I saw an eye, a frightened eye, staring straight back at me. For a few seconds my mind seemed to go blank; it was as if I was being hypnotized. Then the wind blew, rustling the dead leaves, and overhead I heard the distant grumbling of thunder. I glanced up at the darkening sky, pushed the frightened eye deep down inside my trouser pocket, and carried on.

Our house is at the top of the hill, by the road that leads out of Larkstoke village up onto the Wychford Downs. It's a steep hill and some days it feels steeper than others. That particular afternoon it felt almost vertical. We'd had football practice after school and then I'd had to call by Talton Mill farm shop to pick up a bag of potatoes for Mam. It was starting to get dark and people were switching on lights in downstairs rooms. My legs were worn out and the spuds weighed a tonne. I felt like one of those sherpas in the Himalayas, ferrying supplies up the slopes of Mount Everest. *I thought about stopping where I was and establishing Camp Five, but after making radio contact with Base Camp I decided to take my chances and go for the top. The air was thin and cold and the hundred-mile-an-hour winds had sculpted the storm clouds into silver flying saucers that hovered ominously near the summit. At that kind of altitude every step requires a supreme effort; your lungs feel like they're collapsing with each breath; your brain's starved of oxygen and it's not uncommon to start hallucinating, seeing things that aren't really there, like parked cars and stray dogs. You've got to be focused. It's one step after another, each step getting you that little bit higher, that little bit closer.*

Ten minutes later, as the first flurry of snow fell like a shower of sparks from the flying saucers, I stepped through the back door and planted the Union Jack on the ice-clad peak. Mam and Gran were sitting in the kitchen having a cup of tea surrounded by the warm, friendly smell of fresh baking.

'What are those potatoes doing on top of the fridge?' asked Mam.

'I've just climbed Mount Everest. There's a blizzard coming and I've got to get back down before it's too late.'

'You can put them down by the vegetable rack where they normally live, blizzard or no blizzard.'

'Are those cheese scones?'

'They might be,' said Mam, raising her eyebrows superciliously.

'Can I try one?'

'*One.*'

I cradled the cheese scone in the palms of my hands and took a tentative bite.

'*Haa!* They're hot!'

'So would you be if you'd just come out the oven,' said Gran helpfully.

'Have you got my change?' asked Mam.

I put the cheese scone back down and emptied the contents of my pockets onto the kitchen table. There was £3.27 and the frightened eye.

'What's this?' asked Gran, picking it up.

'It's a piece of jigsaw I found on the way home.'

Gran turned it over and for what seemed like ages she stared at the eye while the eye stared back. Mam and I stood in silence waiting for one of Gran's pronouncements. Eventually it came.

'Finding a piece of a jigsaw is a bit like finding a clue.'

'Y . . . e . . . s,' said Mam, like she was trying to understand but didn't really.

'How do you mean, Gran?' I asked.

'The picture can sometimes predict your future. But I'm not sure I like the look of this.'

'Let me see,' said Mam.

Mam took the frightened eye from Gran and studied it carefully.

'I've seen this eye before,' she said mysteriously.

Then she left the kitchen and went into the front room. Half a minute later she came back carrying a big book entitled *The Post-Impressionists*. I'd seen the book before; it was full of pictures of paintings by different artists, most of them French. Mam put it face down on the table and opened it near the back, at the index. She ran her finger down the list of names until she found what she was looking for.

'Redon, Roualt, *Rousseau* ... Henri Rousseau, page 183.'

Page 183 was a painting of some men in stripy bathing suits playing volleyball. I couldn't see the connection. Mam turned over to page 184 and there it was – this amazing painting of a tiger crawling through the jungle. But it wasn't the kind of jungle you might have imagined, all still and spooky with the tiger stealthfully stalking its prey. Instead, there was a howling gale blowing from left to right, tearing leaves from the branches of trees. The rain was coming down in stair rods, you could almost hear it, like millions of dried peas *stotting* off a tin plate. Up at the top you could see streaks of lightning crackling in a steely sky. The tiger looked scared stiff; its eyes were popping out of its head.

'There's your eye,' said Mam, snapping the jigsaw piece down alongside the tiger's head. '*Tiger in a Tropical Storm*; 1891; oil on canvas; The National Gallery, London. It's one of my favourite paintings.'

'Poor old thing,' said Gran. 'No wonder he looks frightened.'

'What's it mean?' I asked, thinking about jigsaw pieces predicting the future.

'All I know for sure,' said Gran, raising her eyebrows, 'is that somewhere there's a one-eyed tiger in a box.'

And that was a whole week before any of us had even heard about Boris – a whole week before it all started.

2

Orion's Belt

Sometimes, when the wind's blowing from the west, or in the stillness of a full moon, you can hear the howler monkeys five miles away in Wychford Zoo. That's something we hadn't reckoned on when we first moved here, but no-one really minds. It's all part of living in the country, or the 'dark interior', as Dad calls it. And anyway, compared to the pheasants and the owls in the Back Wood, the monkeys are as quiet as mice.

We'd lived in Larkstoke for just over a year now and were starting to put down roots. Back in Whitby, Dad had been a fisherman, but now he was a gardener, working for Major Gregory at the Old Manor House. Part of his new job was looking after the pond at the Manor. It was full of the Major's prize koi carp, his 'generals' as he called them. These weren't any old fish. These were prize specimens over a metre long with almost perfect markings, which made them worth a fortune and most of them were even older than Dad!

Mam had opened a craft shop in the village and she was working all hours to try and get it to break even. She'd called it 'Noah's Ark' and not surprisingly it was full of animals. She modelled them out of clay then made a rubber mould and cast them in gleaming white plaster. It was a real production line, each one had a little wire loop sticking out the back so that people could hang them on the wall. The trouble was there weren't that many vacant walls in Larkstoke and the tourist trade had tailed off at the end of August, so business wasn't exactly booming.

One night I was sitting in the front room, wondering why I was watching this moronic game show on telly. We'd all had supper but I was still hungry so I went through to the kitchen to check out the cheese scone situation. The cheese scones were all gone and in their place was a herd of about twenty anaemic-looking zebras. Mam was sitting at the table, squeezing black paint from a tube, getting ready to put them in pyjamas.

'Why so many zebras?' I asked.

"It's a special order for Wychford Zoo, they're going to try and sell them in the zoo shop, see how they go. If they go well there'll be a proper contract with orders for lions, tigers, giraffes . . . you name it.'

'Brilliant!'

'We'll see,' said Mam, stroking the first black stripe across a zebra's bum.

'Where's Dad?'

'Guess.'

I went out the back door and stood at the end of the path. It was pitch black and the sky was alive with stars glistening like the fish scales used to on Dad's black wellies. Lurking behind the trees of the Back Wood, like a giant pumpkin, was a fat orange moon and glowing yellow at the bottom of the garden was Dad's new 'boat' – his greenhouse, adrift on a sea of Brussels sprouts.

I walked up the path and tapped on the glass. Dad slid open the door and I stepped inside.

'Warnings of storms in Dogger,' said Dad, turning off his little radio. 'I wouldn't want to be out there tonight.'

'No,' I said, but I could tell that part of him was still very much 'out there'.

'How's Major Gregory?'

'A bit down,' said Dad. 'I told you Monty died last week?'

'Yes.'

'It seems to have set him back a bit, one of his generals dying of old age. He'll be eighty himself soon. He was asking after you though, said he'd like to see you, three weeks next Sunday, said he'd have something to show you.'

Dad reached down and picked a massive onion from a box on the floor. He held it up to the hurricane lamp that was dangling from the roof and its skin shone golden brown. The full moon rose above the trees and sat there like it was waiting for a push.

'I expect we'll hear the howlers tonight,' he said. 'That full moon'll be getting them all excited.'

'Probably.'

'I was going to start stringing these together tonight,' he said, tossing the onion into the air and catching it again with his other hand, 'but I can't be bothered.'

A large moth suddenly appeared and started dive-bombing the hurricane lamp.

'Come on, let's put this out and take a look at the stars.'

We stepped outside, with the waves of Brussels sprouts brushing against our legs and stood with our heads tilted right back, dizzy with the night.

'It makes you feel so small,' I said. 'There're so many stars.'

'More stars in the sky than grains of sand on the Earth.'

'Is that true?'

'So they reckon.'

'But do you believe it?'

Dad raised his eyebrows and shrugged his shoulders.

'At sea on a boat, that's the place to see stars. Some nights there'd be that many you could hear them sizzle.'

I gave Dad one of Gran's 'hairy eyeball' looks.

'Well, maybe not exactly *sizzle*.'

'Do you know their names?'

'Some of them. You see that group of stars up there, that's the Plough. If you join them together with an imaginary line you can see the handle, the shaft and the share, and if you carry on up from the share you come to Polaris, that's due north. And those five stars close together making the letter W, that's Cassiopeia. And over there's Orion. It's always due south early in the evening, later on it'll move round.'

'It's like a massive compass.'

'It is if you know what you're looking for. See the three stars close together in a straight line?'

'Yes.'

'That's Orion's Belt. They keep his trousers up.'

We started laughing and walked back towards

the house. Halfway down the path Dad stopped and sniffed the air.

'What's that smell?'

'I can't smell anything.'

Dad sniffed again.

'No, it's gone. It was there a few seconds ago, faint but spicy and delicious. Your mam's not cooking anything special is she?'

'Not unless it's zebra stew.'

'No, not zebra. It was more like chicken, or maybe pork. I know, I'll bet it's coming from that new Chinese restaurant, the Red Dragon, that's opened at the top of Church Street. Mmm, I feel hungry. Fancy a bacon sandwich?'

'Not half.'

As we opened the door we heard a faint *whooping* from behind the Back Wood that grew faster and louder then died away.

'The natives are restless tonight,' said Dad, staring into the darkness.

3

Two Wongs

Monday morning was sunny. It's always sunny on a Monday, because that's when you've got to go back to school. I met Billy Gates at the bottom of Church Street. He was waiting for me with Norman. Norman was Billy's dog, a bull terrier with a head on him like a horse. Nearly everyone was scared of Norman, but Norman was like Billy – he just *looked* like a bruiser, he wasn't really. He used to follow Billy to school every day, then walk back home by himself and at home time he'd be there sat outside the school gates, waiting. They were a team.

'*Jimmy!* You'll not believe it!'

'What?'

'They need someone else on a Saturday at the zoo.'

Billy's dad knew the Head Keeper, Frank Wiggins, and Billy spent Saturdays helping out at Wychford Zoo. It wasn't really a 'proper' job, more like work experience, but Frank usually slipped him a tenner and Billy got to go inside some of the cages and feed the animals. Everyone else in the entire school was green with envy. *I* hadn't even been inside the zoo.

'Honest?'

'Yes, honest. Frank says you can start next Saturday.'

'Brilliant!'

'I know. Just think, Jimmy, you and me at the zoo. It'll be like going on safari every Saturday.'

We carried on up Church Street talking animals. Billy didn't talk about much else these days. He wanted to be David Attenborough when he grew up, well, not *actually* David Attenborough, but someone just like him.

'Can you imagine what it's like?' said Billy. 'When you're not on telly you're flying round the world filming everything. One minute you're standing on an iceberg staring at a polar bear and the next minute you're sweating buckets in some tropical rain forest, swatting off giant orange butterflies the size of dustbin lids and picking leeches off your skin 'cos they're sucking your blood. Or maybe vampire bats.'

'Sounds great,' I said, without much conviction.

'It was David Attenborough who filmed those killer whales jumping out of the sea and dragging the seals off the beach, then tossing them in the air and eating them. It was like Friday night outside the chippy, only worse.'

'Billy,' I said.

'Yes?'

'I was thinking. D'you suppose they expect you to have lots of experience with animals?'

'Why?'

''Cos we don't have any pets at home. We've got a bird table round the back and there's an owl comes every night and sits in the tree outside me Gran's window, but that's not like keeping pets.'

'It doesn't matter,' said Billy. 'We've just got Norman. Nothing else.'

We were standing at the top of Church Street outside the Red Dragon waiting for the lights to change.

'Anyway,' says Billy, 'Norman's going to have to stop coming to school.'

'Why's that?'

''Cos of the Chinkies,' said Billy, nodding back towards the Red Dragon. 'My dad says all the dogs in Larkstoke are living on borrowed time. He says, unless they're all kept on a short lead they'll end up in the pot.'

'Don't be daft! That's rubbish. They don't do that.'

'It's true, my dad says. He says he heard about this woman once who went to China on holiday with her pet poodle. She took it in this restaurant, 'cos it went everywhere with her, right. And she wanted something to eat, something for herself and something for the dog. But she didn't speak any Chinese and they didn't speak any English, so she points at the menu, then points at her mouth, then she points at the dog and points at her mouth again. Then guess what?'

'What?' I said flatly, not wanting to hear any more of Billy's nonsense.

'The poodle goes missing, but she thinks it's just gone for a walk and the next thing the waiter comes back with this big silver platter. He lifts off the lid and, *hey presto*, Sweet and Sour Poodle with Pineapple.'

'That's a joke.'

'My dad said it really happened. He said dogs are a delicacy over there.'

'It's Koreans that eat dogs.'

'OK, clever clogs, maybe it was a Korean

restaurant, but the Chinese still eat chicken feet.'

'*What?*'

'You heard, chicken feet. They eat chicken feet. Even *foxes* don't eat the feet, but the Chinkies do. They think it's the best bit.'

'Stop saying "Chinkies", it's stupid. Anyway, the French eat frogs' legs,' I said.

'Yeah, right,' said Billy, 'Arabs eat camels' eyes.'

'And the English eat battered sausages.'

'What's wrong with battered sausages?'

'Nothing. But *they* probably don't think anything's wrong with dogs, or frogs, or chicken feet, or even camels' eyes.'

'You're weird,' said Billy.

The lights had changed and we were standing on the other side of the road. Billy stopped, turned round and looked back at the Red Dragon.

'What about Bird's Nest Soup then?' he asked.

There was no answer to that.

By the time we reached the school gates, we'd been gassing that much, it was nearly nine o'clock. We said goodbye to Norman, dumped our bags and coats and ran along the corridor into the main hall. Everyone else was seated, but there were two empty chairs at the end so we grabbed them. Vivaldi was just getting to the fast bit, where all the violins start to go haywire and right on cue, Mr Ashley, our headmaster, stepped out of his office and strode down to the front to take assembly.

'Go on then,' whispered Billy, nudging me with his elbow. 'What about Bird's Nest Soup?'

I didn't answer. I kept looking straight a head. Firstly, because I didn't want to get caught talking, that meant being kept in at break time, but secondly because I was looking at the back of two heads, two girls' heads, sitting near the front. I'd never seen them before. They both had jet-black hair that was really long and tied back in plaits.

'Go on then. What about it?' pestered Billy.

'Good morning, everyone,' bellowed Mr Ashley.

'Good morning, Mr Ashley,' we all replied.

'Today, I'd like to welcome two new pupils to Larkstoke Junior; Sheila and Sandra Wong.'

4

Blood and Guts

Mam and Dad were chuffed to bits about me starting as a part-time helper at Wychford Zoo. Mam said I had to put a good word in for her zebras and Dad kept whistling this tune from a programme about zoos that used to be on telly donkey's years ago, called *Animal Magic*. Gran was different. When I first told her about the job she looked kind of concerned. She just smiled and nodded, as if she'd known all along. I think she was still a bit worried about the frightened eye, like she saw it as some kind of warning. Personally I didn't read that much into it, I just thought, *Tiger, zoo, part-time job.*

The jigsaw's prediction had come true and my immediate future was sorted.

When Billy called for me on Saturday morning I'd already been up for two hours. I was that excited. We wheeled our bikes down the path and onto the road. The sky was a bright shiny blue. There'd been a bit of a frost during the night and the grass crunched when you walked on it.

'Cor. Brass monkeys, eh?' said Billy, climbing onto his bike. 'Have y'got gloves?'

'Yes,' I said, pulling a pair from the pocket of my fleecy.

'Just as well. 'Cos if y'hadn't we'd need a blow-torch to get your fingers off the handlebars by the time we reached the zoo.'

We set off up Larkstoke Hill, leaving trails of frozen breath streaming behind us. Wychford Zoo was only six miles away, but we were supposed to start at eight o'clock so that meant leaving Larkstoke at seven thirty. The streets were quiet. There was only the postman clattering letter boxes and the milkman clattering bottles.

Ten minutes later we were on the top of the Wychford Downs. It felt like the top of the world. Everything sparkled with dew and down the other side the valley was padded out with soft pillows of mist. It looked like one of those Chinese landscape paintings I'd seen at Major Gregory's house. They were good at mist, the Chinese – misty mountains and koi carp. On either side of us there were sheep in the fields eating turnips. You could hear them munching away and see their breath.

'If this was Africa they'd be wildebeests,' said Billy.

'Or zebras,' I suggested.

'And instead of bikes we'd have armour-plated jeeps in case we got charged by mad rhinos.'

'*Mad rhinos on the horizon!*' I yelled.

'Look! There's the zoo!' shouted Billy, pointing at the tall wooden gates and rooftops that had just begun to emerge through the soft grey.

We started pedalling downhill, getting faster and faster, till all we could hear was the rush of air in our ears and the skin on our faces was pulled tight, the way it does when you're breaking the sound barrier in a supersonic jet.

At the bottom, the road levelled out and we began to slow down. The zoo entrance was about half a mile away, but before you reached it you passed this place on the left that looked like a junk yard with a garden at the front. At first sight, the garden looked ordinary enough with the usual rows of sticks stuck in the ground and tattered bits of netting draped over things to keep the birds off, but when you looked closer you could see this big, enamel bath sitting bang in the middle and in the bath was a naked woman.

You couldn't see her in the summer because of the leaves on the hedges, but in the autumn and winter you could see her quite clearly. Sometimes there'd be cars parked by the side of the road and the drivers would have got out to take a better look and check they weren't seeing things. She wasn't real. She was a shop-window dummy. But it fooled most people.

'Who lives there?' I asked Billy.

'With the woman in the bath?'

'Yes.'

'That's Albert,' he said. 'Daft as a brush.'

Half a minute later we passed a sign propped up by the side of the road.

```
TO LATE!
YOU MISSED IT
TURN ROWND
```

I wanted to ask more, but we were already at the zoo. The main gates were still closed so Billy and I wheeled our bikes in through a smaller, side entrance. I couldn't believe it. I was actually *inside* the zoo! Dad had been promising to take me since we'd first arrived in Larkstoke, but what with one thing and another he'd never got round to it, and now here I was, all set to feed the animals.

'We can leave our bikes over here,' said Billy, walking round the side of a long, low, brick building near the main gates.

'These are the offices. See, "STAFF ONLY". That's us.'

Billy opened a door and I followed him inside to a room with filing cabinets and a small kitchen. On the wall were posters of animals and one of a naked lady riding a motorbike.

'Great pair of wheels, eh?' said Billy, smiling. 'That's Frank's favourite. He'll be around somewhere, but we'd best get started. It's the birds of prey first. "Blood and guts" duty.'

'What's "blood and guts"?' I asked.

'You'll see. Grab a couple of pairs of rubber gloves from the cupboard under the sink. I'll get the brushes and buckets.'

The first cage we came to was the snowy owls. Most of them were huddled in the darkness of their nest box, probably asleep, but one was still awake, sitting in the corner on the floor, all white and watchful, surrounded by blood-spattered bits and pieces. When I stared at him he blinked and shuffled to one side, as though he'd been expecting us.

'This is the blood and guts,' said Billy.

'What happened?'

'Messy eaters, that's all.'

'What do they eat?'

'Frozen chicks mostly. At least they're frozen when the zoo gets them. We thaw them out in the afternoon and feed them to the small carnivores in the evening, after the people have gone. Then we've got to clean up the mess they leave before the people come back the next day. That way no-one gets upset and starts screaming about fluffy chicks getting torn to bits.'

'That's right,' said a voice behind us, 'and I don't expect to find any trace of dismembered chick when I do my rounds at nine o'clock.'

It was the Head Keeper, Frank Wiggins. He wore a grey uniform with a peaked cap. His face was sharp like a weasel's and he had a black moustache that had been trimmed until it was nothing more than a pencil line drawn across his top lip. He pulled a massive set of keys out of his pocket and opened the door to the snowy owl's cage.

'Better look lively. There's all this lot, then the otters.'

'Do otters eat chicks as well?' I asked.

'You'll be the new helper,' said the Head Keeper, jangling the keys in front of my face.

'Yes,' I replied, cautiously.

'Stoker, isn't it?'

I nodded.

'Tell him, Billy,' he said without taking his eyes off my face.

Billy went bright red.

'You're supposed to call the Head Keeper "sir",' he mumbled.

'That's right, "sir". Or, if I'm in a particularly good mood, "Mr Wiggins"'ll do. Now, shall we try again?'

I looked at him, blankly.

'You had a question, Stoker. Or was I imagining things?'

'Please, sir,' I began, trying desperately to remember what it was I'd asked him, 'do the otters . . . eat chicks?'

'Fish and chicks! Every Friday night!' And he started laughing loudly at his own joke until he realized we weren't joining in.

'I've put you both down to clean out the camel enclosure. Watch them, they spit,' he said with a sly grin. 'That should keep you busy till lunchtime. I'm off for a cup of char and a gander at the *Racing Post*. There's a little filly I fancy running in the two thirty at Doncaster. It might be worth a tenner each way. Are you a betting man, Stoker?'

'No, sir.'

'No. You don't look the lucky type.'

He stroked his pencil-line moustache, turned round and walked back towards the offices.

'I hope he wins,' said Billy.

'Why?'

''Cos it'll be our wages up the spout if he doesn't.'

'I see.'

'I'm sorry,' said Billy. 'I should have warned you about Frank ... I mean, Mr Wiggins. He's not normally that bad. My dad says it all depends whose bed he got out of.'

'You mean "which side".'

'No, *whose.*'

After we'd disposed of the blood and guts the visitors started arriving and the whole atmosphere of the zoo was subtly changed. The animals seemed to know what was happening. They all behaved differently; some slunk away out of sight while others appeared from nowhere, pressing their noses against their cages, as if the people were there for their entertainment and not the other way round. Some zoos are depressing, but Wychford was different. The animals had their own space, their own privacy, and it wasn't long before I'd forgotten about Mr Frank Wiggins.

Billy and I spent the next couple of hours mucking out the camels with one of the other keepers, shovelling the business into a big trolley on wheels then pushing it to the dung heap, which was hidden behind some trees in the furthest corner of the zoo. That's something you don't think about when you visit, what happens to the dung. Just like you don't think about all those gory bits and pieces that don't get eaten.

'You've seen the zoo, now here's the poo,' said Billy, pinching his nose with one hand and pointing to the dung heap with the other.

'Herbivores' poo, like the camels' and elephants' isn't that bad. They eat grass and leaves and things. But you should smell the tigers', that stinks! A full-grown tiger eats over two tonnes of meat a year. So you can imagine!'

'Who cleans out the tigers?'

'Frank . . . Mr Wiggins,' said Billy with a smile. 'He hates it, but he's the only one allowed in there, him and the Director, Mr Wainwright. They won't let us anywhere near them, not even when they're locked away inside their sleeping quarters. It's too dangerous. Frank knew someone at this other zoo had his whole arm bitten off. He was trying to clean up, but the tiger thought he was trying to pinch his food. Tigers don't like to share.'

'I haven't seen the tigers,' I said.

'They're awesome. C'mon, I'll show you.'

The zoo was enormous with lots of hedges and winding paths. If you wanted to find something in particular you needed a map or you'd be walking round for hours. It was more like a maze full of animals. The tiger enclosure was at the southernmost end, surrounded by two wire fences. A high one, that was bent over at the top, to keep the tigers in and a low one, set back round the outside, to keep the visitors from getting too close.

The enclosure was full of trees and bushes like a proper jungle and there was even a pool of water for them to swim in, but when you saw the size of the tigers you knew why they needed the space. They were Siberian tigers from the far east of Russia, the biggest tigers in the world. They were stretched out on the grass in front of the pool, looking like they belonged on another planet. They were big, beautiful, and scary.

'The smaller one's called Olga,' said Billy. 'She's ten years old. The big one's Boris, he's nearly twenty. That's ancient. Boris can't walk properly anymore 'cos he's got rheumatism in his legs and he can't see properly either 'cos he's got cataracts on his eyes. They've tried operating, but it's no use. He's totally blind in one eye and the other's not much use. Frank reckons he won't last much longer.'

I stared at the one-eyed tiger and for a short while he seemed to stare back. My mind went blank, as if I was being hypnotized, then he flicked his tail and turned away.

5

Albert Spark

On Sunday night, Boris died.

Billy told me when he saw me at school on the Monday morning. Frank Wiggins had told Billy's dad, and he'd told Billy, so it had to be true.

I knew it was on the cards, just from what Billy had said was wrong with him, but I still felt sad – sad and strange, because Gran's prediction had come true and now I was wondering what else might happen. I decided to keep quiet about Boris. Whatever it was, I'd deal with it myself.

At school I tried to make friends with the Wong sisters, Sheila and Sandra. They were new and I still remembered how that felt. It must have been twice as hard for them, because they weren't just from a different part of England, they were Chinese. But they were twins, so maybe that evened things out.

Their dad owned the Red Dragon restaurant on Church Street. They'd been living in London with their mum and had just moved to Larkstoke. They spoke English with a London accent and also Chinese. They spoke Chinese to each other, like a secret language. When I first tried talking to them they'd both start giggling and run away. It was dead embarrassing, but then I got the chance to tell them about Major Gregory and his famous collection of koi carp. That stopped them giggling. Then I told them about the zoo and how Boris the Siberian tiger had just died. That got them interested and they started asking questions, but then Billy came along and it scared them off.

Nothing much happened the rest of the week and before I knew it, it was Saturday and Billy and I were being chased by mad rhinos again down Wychford Hill. We were a bit late, because Norman had got out the house and followed Billy. He wouldn't go home by himself, so we had to take him. There was no mist this time. It was warmer and the sky was all hazy with a thin layer of cloud. The naked lady was still in the bath and there was a big man in red overalls with a huge, bushy black beard standing beside her. The man was real.

Frank Wiggins was waiting for us by the main gates.

'You're late,' he said.

'We had to take Norman back, Mr Wiggins,' said Billy. 'He followed us.'

'It's five past eight.'

'Sorry, sir,' I said.

Frank Wiggins stared at me, narrowing his eyes till they were just slits, trying to decide whether I was being sarcastic.

' "Blood and guts" then, first thing,' he said, sounding like it was some kind of treat. 'But you've both missed the real blood and guts.'

'You mean Boris?' said Billy.

'No, the flamingos.'

'What happened, sir?' I asked.

He stopped and looked at me again, as if he'd forgotten what he was going to say.

'With the flamingos, Mr Wiggins,' prompted Billy.

'Couple of foxes,' said the Head Keeper, brightening up. 'They got under the wire fence of the flamingo enclosure and had a party.'

'Did they . . .' began Billy.

'Six, at two thousand quid a piece. That's twelve thousand quid in one night. Stupid birds can't fly 'cos they've had their wings clipped, see. They must have just stood on those daft long legs of theirs, like sticks of candy floss.'

'Didn't anyone hear them?' I asked, deciding to drop the "sir"?'

'It was night-time, Stoker. There's no-one in the zoo at night,' he sneered. 'But you should have seen the mess this morning. They're still picking feathers out of the lake. What's left of the birds is in the freezer with Boris and a couple of penguins that pegged it at the same time. Wainwright's having the fence electrified. It's going to cost a bomb, but I suppose it's cheaper to *fry* the foxes than feed them flamingos.'

He started laughing. Billy started laughing too, but I didn't think it was that funny.

'I suppose it's been a bad week for Wychford Zoo, what with old Boris and then the flamingos,' he continued, running his finger one way then the other over his pencil-line moustache. 'Still, mustn't grumble. There's a smart bit of totty coming along later to try and make a tape recording of Olga growling. It's probably for some television documentary and if she plays her cards right I might just give her the benefit of my years of experience handling tigers.'

We both must have looked particularly unimpressed.

'I'm knocking a quid off each of your wages for being late. *Move it!*'

'Yes, sir.'

We got the blood and guts out of the way, mucked out the llamas and zebras, and then fed the howlers. The rest of the day we were on litter duty, walking round in circles picking up discarded paper cups, sticky sweet wrappers and, worst of all, chewing gum. It was amazing how many people chewed gum. In some places the black asphalt path looked like a map of the night sky. But it wasn't as tedious as it sounds, there were always the animals to watch, and that included the people. Some of them were just as entertaining, like Frank Wiggins, who spent most of the afternoon pestering the lady who'd come to tape record Olga growling. I guess he was trying to impress her with his vast experience of handling tigers. Billy and I kept our distance but, from what we could see either she wasn't playing her cards right or she was even less impressed than we were.

At half past four it was time to go home and we were halfway out the main gates when Frank Wiggins called us back.

'Aren't you two forgetting something?'

Me and Billy looked at each other blankly and I had visions of being marched back to muck out the elephant house.

'I don't think so, sir,' I said, warily.

'Forget the "sir" business, Jim lad. Here, this is for both of you and there's a bit extra in there too.'

And he handed me a plain brown envelope. I was speechless.

'There's just one little favour I'd like you to do.'

'Yes?'

'Y'see those black plastic bags over by the bins?'

'Yes.'

'I'd like you to drop them off at Albert Spark's place. He'll be expecting you.'

'No problem,' said Billy, wheeling his bike back inside the main gates.

I followed him and together we hoisted the bags, one onto each set of handlebars. They were very heavy and even though they were knotted at the top there was a seriously unpleasant smell enveloping each bag. When we were well out of earshot I turned to Billy.

'*Phworrrr!* What's in these?' I gasped.

'I don't know. Smells like something dead. What's in the envelope?'

I opened the envelope and pulled out twenty-five quid.

'Blimey!' said Billy. 'What's happened to him?'

'Maybe he was feeling generous,' I suggested.

'Doubt it. More likely he picked a winner from the *Racing Post*.'

We pushed the bikes keeping our noses as far away from the bags as possible.

'How far do we have to carry them?' I asked.

'Just up the road.'

'Who's Albert Spark?'

'The man with the naked lady in the bath,' said Billy.

'Is that all he does? Put odd things in his garden?'

'No, he does all sorts. My dad says he's got more fingers in more pies than anyone else around. The trouble is, they're not always *his* pies. He's a bit dodgy. You've got to watch him. My dad says he's been inside.'

'Inside where?' I asked, naively.

'Inside the nick – prison. My dad says he'd sell his granny for a couple of quid. He used to run a pub called The Monkey and Drum, but the brewery chucked him out 'cos he was watering down the beer. When they first caught him he said the beer was watery because the roof leaked, and it'd been raining a lot. He got away with a caution that time.'

By the time we reached the junk yard I was feeling kind of nervous. Albert Spark was sitting on an old tractor tyre, leaning over two large squares of plywood that were lying on the ground. He had long, black, curly hair that was going grey at the ends, and a beard that came halfway down his chest. His red overalls were covered in grease and he was holding a paintbrush in his right hand. The paintbrush was quite big, but in *his* hands, with fingers the size of bananas, it looked like one of those my mam used for painting the stripes on her plaster zebras. When he heard us coming he looked up with eyes that seemed to be looking in two completely different directions.

'Ay up, lads, I could smell th' coming half mile away. I suppose that lot's for me.'

'Frank sent them,' said Billy. 'They stink!'

'That's the general idea,' laughed Albert Spark.

'So what's in them?' asked Billy.

'Tiger muck, lad. One hundred per cent pure tiger muck.'

'What for?'

'It were Frank spotted it. He saw this article in some fancy gardening magazine about how tiger muck's the business for sorting out cats.'

'Cats?'

'Aye, y'know how folk get their knickers in a twist about stray cats scrattin' around their flower beds. Well, a few dollops of tiger muck scattered here and there seems t'do the trick. One sniff and they're off.'

'Can't say I blame them,' I muttered.

'Billy Gates, where's yer manners? Y've not introduced yer friend.'

'Sorry, Albert. This is Jimmy, Jimmy Stoker.'

'Albert Spark, at yer service.'

And he held out a massive hand completely engulfing my own. I was waiting for the bones to start cracking, but he just gave a gentle squeeze.

'Pleased to meet you, Mr Spark.'

'Forget the "Mr Spark" bit, lad. It's plain old Albert, nowt else,' he said, dropping his hand and rubbing at a drip of black paint that had spilt on the leg of his overalls.

'You're not from round these parts,' he continued.

'I live in Larkstoke.'

'Aye, but y'haven't always lived in Larkstoke. Not with an accent like that.'

'I'm from Whitby.'

'*Whitby*. Grand place. What brought you to this neck of the woods?'

'Me dad was a fisherman, but he packed it in.'

'Aye, it's a hard life being a fisherman,' mused Albert, thoughtfully. 'Always was, and it's not got any better.'

He put the lid on a can of black paint then leant forward and lifted up the squares of plywood so that they were standing on their ends. 'Whatd'y'think?' he asked. Billy and I stepped round behind him so we could see.

```
┌─────────────────────────────────┐
│                                 │
│   FED UP WITH SCRATIN           │
│         CATS?                   │
│   PUT A TIGER IN                │
│     YER GARDEN!                 │
│                                 │
└─────────────────────────────────┘
```

```
┌─────────────────────────────────┐
│                                 │
│   Genuin Tiger Muck             │
│      for Sale                   │
│  (one wif and there off!)       │
│                                 │
└─────────────────────────────────┘
```

'You see, the idea's to spread it out a bit,' said Albert.

'What? The tiger muck?' said Billy.

'No, yer daft barmpot, the signs. You don't want too many words on the one sign else folks will miss it. They're in their cars. You've got to catch their eye with the first one, get them thinking, and then explain things with the second, which you put further down the road. I reckon about thirty yards is about right for a car travelling at normal speed. There was this programme on telly, and in Los

42

Angeles these huge shops have one word in each window so that folks driving past can read a sentence. If you were walking past it probably wouldn't make any sense, but them Americans drive everywhere. Daft as dormice.'

'I see,' said Billy, not entirely convincingly.

'Aye, it's all clever stuff,' said Albert. 'But this tiger muck could be a nice little earner for me and Frank.'

'How much are you selling it for?' I asked.

'A fiver a bag.'

'But Frank gave us a fiver for fetching it,' said Billy.

'We're not selling *these* bags for a fiver,' laughed Albert. 'Tiger muck's like expensive perfume; a little goes a long way. I've a stack of smaller bags round the back and I reckon one of these'll fill twenty of the others.'

'So that's two hundred quids' worth,' I said, staring at the two smelly bags we'd carried up from the zoo.

'That's right, Jim lad. It's like they say, "Where there's muck there's brass!" Mind, if what Frank says is right, the real money's not in them bags. It's down there, in the freezer.'

'How d'y'mean?' I asked.

'Yon tiger that popped his clogs. Frank tells me it's worth thousands on the black market.'

43

'You mean the skin?' said Billy.

'Aye, there's the skin. That's meant to be worth a fiver a square inch. And yon tiger's a big lad. But it's not just the skin. There's summat else. It's the *bones*. Frank says they're even more valuable than the skin. He says the Chinese grind them down and make ointments and potions and such for curing things like arthritis.'

'But Boris had arthritis,' I said.

'Makes no odds,' said Albert, 'tiger bones is tiger bones and them Chinese pay top dollar.'

'That's why there's hardly any tigers left,' said Billy. ' 'Cos the Chinkies are eating them all.'

'Don't be daft!' I said.

'I'm not being daft.'

'There must be other reasons.'

'Like what?'

'I don't know.'

'Well I do,' said Billy. My dad says it's all because of the Chinkies. It's the same with rhinoceroses. They eat the horns. And sharks, 'cos they eat the fins.'

'Daft as dormice,' muttered Albert, shaking his head. 'Still, it's a right shame yon tiger's dead. There's only one now and that means half the muck.'

'What do you think they'll do with Boris?' I asked, suddenly thinking of him lying frozen

44

in the zoo freezer.

'Probably bury him,' said Billy.

'That's not what Frank says,' said Albert.

We both looked at him, waiting for an explanation.

'There's plans. But it's all a bit hush-hush. "Three Wise Monkeys", know what I mean?'

We didn't talk much on the way back. I guess we were both pondering the fate of Boris. Billy raced off ahead, which was fine by me. He was getting on my nerves, anyway. The way he kept on about the Chinese, saying how they all ate tigers, and rhinos, and dogs. Maybe *some* of them did, but it was the way he said it – the way he implied they were all the same, the way he called them 'Chinkies'. I knew it was only a matter of time before the muck hit the fan.

6

The Final Straw

'Checkmate,' said Sheila Wong.

I stared at the board. She was right. I couldn't believe it. We'd only just started the game and she'd beaten me.

'How did you do that?' I asked.

'Kieseritzky's Gambit,' she said. 'He was a Russian Grand Master. It was a trap and you fell for it. White moves pawn to king's bishop 4; black does the same; white knight to king's bishop 3; black pawn to knight 4 . . . Do you want me to go on?'

'No . . . It's OK,' I said, trying to sound like I understood what had happened. 'Do you fancy another game?'

'Sure. But this time you play Sandra.'

I set up the pieces on the board while Sheila got up and Sandra sat down. Sheila and Sandra Wong had joined the school chess club and so far no-one had been able to beat them. It was Wednesday lunchtime and the school library was quiet, except for the noise of the rain on the windows and the occasional *click* of a wooden chess piece.

The start of the second game was less dramatic and twenty minutes later I thought I was ahead. I thought about sacrificing my knight in the hope that she'd leave her king open to check and then maybe mate. I looked up at Sandra, trying to guess whether she knew what I was planning, but her expression remained totally inscrutable. So I looked up at Sheila, who was standing right behind her, looking down at the board. No difference. Neither of them had said a word since the first move. It was like playing against a computer. Two computers.

I decided to risk it. I moved my knight and she took it like I'd hoped. Check. *Yes!* But then her queen appeared out of nowhere. Checkmate. I'd lost.

'Was that another Russian gambit?' I asked.

'No. That was Chinese. The "Wong Way".'

We all started laughing.

'What sign are you?' asked Sheila.

'What do you mean?'

'Star sign. When's your birthday?'

'November 29th,' I said.

'Sagittarius,' said Sheila. 'That makes you a rat.'

'Thanks a bunch.'

'No, silly,' laughed Sandra. 'Rats are good. In Chinese astrology everyone is a different animal. There are horses, dogs, monkeys – even dragons.'

'What are you?'

'We're dragons.'

'I'd rather be a dragon than a rat,' I said.

'You can never be a dragon,' said Sheila. 'You will always be a rat. You are a rat firstly because of the year you were born. And secondly because of the date. Do you know the exact time of day you were born?'

'No. Why?'

'That also determines which animal you are. Sandra and I are also rats and horses, but mostly dragons. You are a rat on two counts, so I'd say that's pretty definite. But you should be happy to be a rat.'

'How come?'

'Rats are considered to be quick-witted, adaptable and good at games, like chess.'

'I'd have thought that ruled me out,' I said, feeling slightly embarrassed. 'What's the downside of being a rat?'

'They're sly,' said Sandra.

'And careless,' added Sheila.

'That sounds more like it,' I laughed.

'What about your friend?' said Sandra. 'The boy you work with at the zoo.'

'Billy?'

'Yes. When's *his* birthday?'

'I think it's November 12th.'

'Scorpio,' said Sheila. 'He's a pig.'

The door swung upon and Billy stood at the end of the library with Sam Warner. They walked towards us, slowly.

'What's up, Billy?' I asked, scooping the chess pieces back into the box.

'Just wanted to tell you something,' said Billy, looking sideways at Sheila and Sandra.

'In *private*,' sneered Sam.

'Yeah. No offence girls,' said Billy, 'but we don't want any *Chinese whispers*. Know what I mean?'

Billy and Sam started laughing and I felt myself getting hot and angry.

'That's OK,' said Sheila quietly. 'We were going anyway.'

They put the board away and left in silence. Billy and Sam watched them go with big, stupid smiles on their faces. Then Billy turned to me.

'What're y'talking to those two about?'

'Pigs,' I said, trying to keep calm.

'*Pigs?*' echoed Sam.

'They're everywhere, you know,' said Billy.

'What do you mean?' I asked.

'Chinkies. There's another one opening in Wychford.'

'Big deal. So what,' I said.

'So. They're taking over the world. My dad says there's more Chinkies than anybody else. He says there's *billions*. He says there's that many that they've had to stop having babies. And if they do have a baby they get put in prison.'

'It's the "Yellow Peril",' said Sam Warner, pulling back the corners of his eyes with his fingers and sticking out his front teeth.

'It's true,' said Billy. 'My dad says . . .'

'*Billy,*' I said. And he stopped. 'Your dad says a lot of things. And most of them are total rubbish. If you can't find anything better to do than stir up trouble for Sheila and Sandra, you can count me out.'

'What's the matter. D'y'fancy them, or something?' sneered Sam.

I didn't say anything. I put the box of chess pieces down on the table and stepped forwards. Sam stepped back, looking worried, but I kept walking, across the library and out of the door.

'I was going to tell you a secret,' shouted Billy.

'Stuff your secret!' I shouted back.

*

The rest of the week was predictably bad. Sam Warner had gone round the whole school telling people that I fancied the Wong sisters. I wanted to grab him and punch his face in. But I didn't. I decided to bide my time and wait till next Saturday. I was sure that when it was just me and Billy we'd sort things out. He'd have had time to think about what I'd said and I'd have had time to calm down. But on Saturday morning there was no Billy. I waited outside on the road till twenty to eight, then I ran back inside and phoned his number. It was his dad who answered.

'Billy's not going to the zoo today. He's coming shooting with me instead.'

'Shooting what?' I asked, half expecting him to say 'Chinkies'.

'Pheasants,' he said. And hung up.

Thanks a bunch, I thought. Thanks for telling me!

I ran back outside and jumped on my bike. It was now a quarter to eight. I had fifteen minutes to make the zoo – no chance! I pedalled like the clappers, but it was ten past eight when I skidded to a halt outside the main gates. Frank Wiggins was waiting for me.

'Ten minutes late. You're pushing it aren't you, Stoker?'

'Sorry, sir,' I panted.

'Never mind, at least you're here. That's more than can be said of some.'

'Billy's . . .'

'Got better things to do,' he interrupted, 'like shooting defenceless birds.'

I kept quiet.

'Makes no odds. One less wage for me to pay, but twice the work for you to do.'

'I'll get started then, sir.'

'Better had. And Stoker . . .'

'Yes, sir?'

'Let's drop the "sir". For today.'

I kept busy and the day passed quickly. By the time I'd finished it wasn't exactly dark, but really grey and dull. The nights were starting to pull in and there was a thick fog hanging in the air. Nearly everyone had left the zoo, even though there was still half an hour before closing. I walked over to the zoo shop and peered through the window to see if I could spot Mam's zebras. I couldn't see much, so I went inside and looked round. There was everything from penguin pencil sharpeners to hippopotamus hot-water-bottle covers, but there wasn't a single plaster zebra in sight. My heart sank. They'd obviously decided not to sell them.

'Can I help you?' asked the lady behind the counter.

'I was looking for a plaster zebra,' I said.

'You're too late. I sold the last one this morning. They've been *ever* so popular. I'm sure we'll be getting some more in soon.'

'Great!' I said. And meant it.

That really cheered me up. So I didn't mind when I met Frank Wiggins outside and he presented me with an enormous bag of tiger poo.

'Just the one this week. Tell Albert, he'll have to make it spin out. And here's fifteen quid – a tenner for the day's work and a fiver for running the errand.'

'Thanks, Mr Wiggins!'

'Don't mention it, lad. Remember ... it's between us.'

Fifteen quid! I couldn't believe it. A few weeks ago I'd have happily paid a fiver just to get into the zoo and now they were paying me a tenner for being there. The extra fiver was the icing on the cake. I left straightaway and it wasn't until I reached Albert's place that I realized I'd left my gloves back at the zoo. Albert was over by the far shed surrounded by a disorderly pile of small plastic bags.

'Aye up, Jim lad. Is that what I think it is?'

'Frank says there's only the one this week and you've to spin it out.'

'Good old Frank. Sharp as Sheffield that lad. He dropped the other bag by yesterday,' said Albert, nodding at a much larger plastic bag round the corner.

'What's in there?' I asked.

'Donkey muck. I'm mixing it fifty-fifty with the tiger's.'

'Are cats scared of donkeys?'

'Probably not. But it's just till supplies return to normal.'

'Can't you use lions'?' I asked.

'Someone else mucks out the lions.'

'*Leopards?*' I suggested.

'Leopards are constipated,' said Albert, despondently. 'It's a fickle business, the muck business. Y've got to be creative to stay on top of pile. Now, drop that bag down here and give us a hand fillin'.'

'I can't stay, Albert. I've left my gloves at the zoo. I'll have to get back there before they close. And besides, it'll be dark soon and the light on me bike's gone on the blink.'

'Bulb or battery?'

'Bulb, I think.'

'Fetch th' bike,' said Albert, rising to his feet and setting off towards the far end of the junkyard, where two old railway carriages stood end to end surrounded by wrecked cars. The whole place looked like a major disaster area. Albert disappeared through the door of the first railway carriage, then reappeared ten seconds later.

'Look lively. Y'll miss the train.'

I stepped up and followed him inside.

'Welcome to "Spark Hall",' said Albert. 'Now, what was it we were after? Bulbs? They'll be through in the north wing.'

We walked the length of the carriage, through the dividing doors, into the next one. Most of the seats had been taken out and there was a crazy patchwork of old carpets covering the floor. The windows were either boarded up or had curtains drawn across, so it was really gloomy. Albert flicked a switch and a yellow light shone down from the ceiling.

'All mod cons,' he said proudly.

Suddenly the carriage looked warm and cosy.

'Is this where you live?' I asked.

'Just in the winter,' replied Albert. 'In the summer it's usually the villa in Monte Carlo or the yacht in the Seychelles.' And he gave me a wink. 'What d'y'think?'

'Great,' I said, looking round and pausing at a poster of a naked lady riding a motorbike.

'Aye. It were Frank gave me that,' said Albert, sounding slightly embarrassed. 'Bulbs are over here.'

He reached up to a shelf that was laden with rusty tin cans and started lifting them down, one by one, peering inside and poking at contents with his stubby forefinger.

'Nails . . . screws . . . washers . . . bicycle clips . . . *bulbs*!'

He unscrewed the front of my lamp and extracted the tiny bulb, holding it up to his ear and shaking it.

'Dead,' he said, emphatically.

Then he put his fingers into the rusty tin can and stirred round the tiny glass bulbs until he found one that looked the same. He screwed it into the lamp, illuminating his grimy fingers.

'Thanks, Albert,' I said.

'Don't mention it, lad. There's nowt that Albert Spark can't fettle.'

'I'd best get going.'

'Aye, and watch the roads. That fog's getting thicker by the minute.'

I left Albert and pedalled slowly down the road, back towards the zoo. The beam of my lamp seemed to be stuck in the swirling grey fog and I couldn't see that well, but I figured I was all right because other people would be able to see me. Up ahead there were two red lights and voices, so I slowed right down, then stopped. The red lights were the tail lights of a large white van parked outside the zoo and the voices were coming from just inside the zoo entrance. One of them was a woman's and another was Frank Wiggins.

I stood dead still and switched off my lamp. Someone came out and opened the back doors of the van. Then the others came out, carrying something heavy. Everything was blurred and grey with fog, but I could see that the thing they were carrying was wrapped in a blanket, but only round its body. Its head, and its feet, and its tail, were sticking out – frozen stiff and motionless.

It was Boris.

The back doors of the van slammed shut and someone climbed in the front. The engine revved noisily and the van slowly turned round. I dragged my bike off the road and hid behind a hedge. The driver changed from first to second as the van sped past in the fog. But not before I'd read the wording on the side of the van. It said *Red Dragon Chinese Restaurant*.

7

The Tiger Hunt

That night I couldn't get to sleep, not for ages.
When I did eventually drift off I had this
nightmare.

*I was sitting in the back of the white van with Boris.
There was a chess board on the floor, covered with all the
pieces. I kept saying, 'Come on Boris! It's your move!'
But he just sat there, staring into space. The doors of the
van suddenly opened and there were Sheila and Sandra,
dressed up as chefs, standing in the middle of a huge, red
kitchen. Frank Wiggins was there too, sharpening a
giant meat cleaver. They were all talking in Chinese and
no–one seemed to have noticed me. Then the girls reached*

58

into the van and pulled out Boris, dragging him across the floor towards a massive cauldron of boiling water. I shouted, 'Stop!' and they all slowly turned to look at me. 'It's Jimmy,' said one of the girls. 'Jimmy the rat. He's lost the game of chess and now he has to pay the price.'

'Put him in the pot!' shouted Frank Wiggins.

They all came into the back of the van.

And that's when I woke up, lying across the bed, with the sheets wrapped round my ankles.

'They didn't have any cornflakes,' said Mam, sliding the packet of Frosties across the breakfast table.

I stared at the cartoon of the tiger on the front and my mind went blank.

'Don't you like Frosties?' she asked.

'They're fine,' I said, trying to act normal and pouring myself a double helping into a bowl.

Gran sat opposite scraping burnt bits off a piece of toast.

'What does it mean, Gran, when you dream about tigers?' I asked.

She stopped scraping and gave me a serious look.

'Tigers are a warning to stay out of trouble.'

'Just wondered,' I said, waiting for the inquisition.

'You'll be off to see Major Gregory this morning,' said Dad, coming to the rescue.

'Yes. What time's he expecting me?'

'Ten o'clock I think. Best look sharp. You know what a stickler he is for punctuality.'

I shovelled down the Frosties and grabbed my fleecy. It looked cold outside.

'Jimmy,' said Gran, as I opened the back door. 'Tell Major Gregory I think it's a good idea.'

I was going to ask her *what* was a good idea, but she started scraping again. I left her smiling at her black speckled plate, wondering whether she could 'read' the burnt toast the same way she could 'read' the tea leaves.

It had been ages since I'd seen the Major and I was really looking forward to it. He was the first friend I made when we moved to Larkstoke. And now, with Dad working at the Manor, we'd sort of adopted him as part of the family. I could talk to him about anything and he'd listen. It didn't seem to matter about him being old and living in a posh house.

Sometimes he'd come round for supper and afterwards we'd all sit round the fire and listen to his stories. They always began the same way: '*When I was in the war . . .*' And then he'd go on about the different battles he'd been in. Not boasting, just reminiscing. One thing leading to another, so that he might begin sitting in a tank somewhere in the desert and end up talking about how Eskimos catch whales. It was better than the telly. Everyone was fascinated – everyone except Gran, who'd always get up and go through to the kitchen muttering something like, '*He's off again!*' But that never stopped him. In fact, it seemed to spur him on.

The Old Manor House was right in the middle of the village and I had my own key to a door in the wall by the stream, that opened onto the garden. The Major was standing over by the big pond, staring at the ground. The soft grass smothered the sound of my footsteps and it wasn't until I was right beside him that he noticed me.

'Ah, James,' he said, wiping what looked like a tear from his cheek. 'Glad you're here. I was just beginning to get a trifle sentimental, thinking of . . .'

He didn't finish the sentence, but tapped at the tiny gravestone of General Patton with the brass tip of his walking stick. General Patton had been the Major's favourite koi carp. He'd died 'in action' last year, somewhere between Larkstoke and Dover.

'I was sorry to hear about General Montgomery,' I said.

'Yes. Him too,' he sighed. 'But time marches on, and none of us are getting any younger. I was going to bury Monty alongside General Patton here, but those two old coves never did see eye to eye. In the end, I thought it best to keep them apart.'

'What did you do with him?'

'Ah, that's my little surprise. I had him stuffed.'

'*Stuffed!*'

'Quite so. But we're not supposed to use that word,' he whispered, bending forward and glancing over his shoulder. 'Taxidermists don't like it, you know. It's all very technical, but apparently it has nothing to do with "stuffing" whatsoever. My good friend, Kit, informs me that stuffing is what one does to teddy bears and turkeys. The correct terminology is "mounted".'

'Can I see?'

'Of course, dear boy. Follow me.'

There were more rooms in the Major's house than there were houses in Larkstoke. You could spend the whole day walking round the place. But my favourite room of all was his study. It was crammed full of interesting things, mostly either Chinese or Japanese, and mostly to do with koi carp. That's where Monty was hanging, floating in mid air about half a metre above a red lacquered Chinese sideboard. I'd expected to find him in a box, but the Major had him suspended from the ceiling using two lengths of almost invisible fishing line. When we walked in, the draught from opening the door made him wiggle. It was totally eerie, watching him swim through the air like that. I kept expecting him to open his lips and bubbles to come out. Everything was there. Everything was perfect. Like the first day I saw him.

'What do you think?' asked the Major.

'Amazing!'

'I thought I'd let him swim around the study for a while. Stretch his old fins one last time.'

'Aren't you going to put him in a box?'

'As a matter of fact I'm having a special oak display case made, but it's not quite ready. Eventually he'll be behind glass, above the fireplace in the reception room, keeping an eye on things.

'When I first broached the subject Kit tried to dissuade me from having him mounted. As a rule, taxidermists prefer not to do pets. She said what I really wanted was to have him alive and well and swimming in the pond, not on display. But when I explained about Monty and General Patton being such odd bedfellows she finally agreed.'

We sat down on the sofa and drank tea from china cups. There were waterlilies painted round the rim and when I'd finished I saw a bright orange koi carp lurking in the dregs at the bottom.

'How's the family?' asked the Major.

'Fine.'

'And your grandmother?'

'Oh, she said to tell you it was a good idea.'

'Excellent!' exclaimed the Major, placing his cup and saucer on the table. 'That's . . .' He seemed to be holding his breath. 'Excellent!'

'*What*'s a good idea?' I asked, totally bemused.

'A bit of a celebration. A joint birthday party of sorts. Mine's on November 6th and your grandmother's is on November 4th. We thought we'd do something here at the Manor, on November 5th.'

'Bonfire Night?'

'Precisely. There's heaps of dead wood in the garden, enough to build a splendid bonfire and, as for catering, I thought we might try something a bit different. Have you noticed we now have a Chinese restaurant in Larkstoke?'

'Yes, the Red Dragon.'

'Indeed, the Red Dragon. Your grandmother and I had a first-rate meal there last Wednesday evening and discussed the possibility of them laying on a suitably lavish spread here at the Manor for November 5th.'

'*You had dinner with Gran?*'

'Well, yes. Didn't she mention it?'

'I didn't even know she liked Chinese food.'

'A lady of refined tastes, your grandmother.'

I nodded, thinking about Gran and her battered sausages.

'Do *you* like Chinese food?' asked the Major.

'Me? I'll try anything once.'

'That's the ticket! Personally I'm rather partial to those little steamed dumplings stuffed with duck and plum sauce. Can't imagine how they make them so "more-ish". Devilishly clever people. Did you know it was the Chinese who first invented the compass? Not to mention paper and gunpowder. And, speaking of Bonfire Night, fireworks! Now, there's an idea.'

This was all great news, but I wasn't thinking of Bonfire Night, I was thinking of tigers.

'Is it true that Chinese people eat tigers?' I asked.

'I can't say I noticed it on the menu.'

'No, I mean, is it true that in China they use the bones and things to make medicines?'

The Major tilted his head back and nodded slowly, then made himself comfortable on the sofa.

'The tiger is a protected animal. And in modern-day China, the killing of tigers is against the law. But at the same time, the tiger is associated with tremendous energy and power and sadly there are unscrupulous people *throughout* the world who are prepared to kill tigers in order to exploit the myths that surround them. Even today, in China, there are millions of people who remain utterly convinced that tiger bones possess extraordinary curative powers.'

'But that's daft!'

'Strange, but not necessarily "daft". After all,

who would have thought, a hundred and fifty years ago, that a humble piece of mould would hold the secret to penicillin. And Chinese medicine is thousands of years older than our own, but to most Westerners it remains as mysterious as the moon. I think it is wrong to dismiss what we don't understand.'

'So, do you think it works?'

'*Something* works. And that is indeed unfortunate for the poor tigers. The task ahead is to find a less costly substitute and save the tigers' skins . . . and bones! But what has prompted this sudden interest in *Panthera tigris*?'

'You know I've got this Saturday job, helping at the zoo?'

'Yes, I was going to ask you about that.'

'Well, there's this tiger there called Boris. At least, there *was* this tiger there called Boris. He died a couple of weeks ago.'

'So I heard.'

'I went back to the zoo last night, just after it had closed. I'd left my gloves in the office. It was foggy and I couldn't see much, but I saw this white van parked outside and some people putting something in the back. It was Boris.'

'Aha! And you think the dead tiger has been stolen by some dastardly, Chinese tiger bone thief.'

'*No*. It's just . . .'

'Put your mind at rest, dear boy,' said the Major, removing his little round gold spectacles and polishing them with a spotted handkerchief which he kept tucked in the breast pocket of his tweed jacket. 'Let me make a quick telephone call. And then, I fancy, we'll go on a tiger hunt.'

Ten minutes later we were belting along in the Major's old Land Rover, down Wychford Hill towards the zoo. I knew he had something up his sleeve, but he wasn't letting on. He just kept talking about how autumn was his favourite time of year, muttering about 'mists' and 'mellow fruitfulness'. When we drove past Albert's place there was another new sign by the side of the road.

CATS TODAY, GON TOMOORA! SPARKS TIGER MUCK dus the trick!

'Curious,' said the Major, slowing down.

I was expecting him to stop at the zoo. Instead

he drove straight past. He must have seen me looking puzzled because he turned round and said, 'Not far now,' and a couple of minutes later he pulled off the road and parked beside a large, derelict building set back in the trees.

It looked like it had been empty for years, like that castle in the story of Sleeping Beauty. It was surrounded by a high wire fence, but the gate was wide open and hanging off its hinges. A sign on the gate said: THESE PREMISES ARE THE PROPERTY OF THE BRAINE'S GLUE COMPANY. TRESPASSERS WILL BE PROSECUTED.

'Dangerous territory!' whispered the Major, as he glanced over his shoulder and stepped inside.

I followed him.

A tall, red-bricked chimney that had seen better days poked out of the roof at the far end. Some of the windows were cracked and there were slates missing off the roof. An old wooden sign that was shaped like a pot of glue and said BRAINE'S GLUE BONDS BRITAIN in faded black letters had fallen off the wall and lay face up on the ground, half hidden by nettles and willow herb.

There was a door near the road, but someone had nailed wooden planks and metal bars across it. Probably the same person who had put wire mesh over the rest of the windows, to stop people chucking stones and breaking the glass. The Major walked past the boarded-up door, turned the corner and walked along the wall to a rusty old fire escape. At the bottom was a mailbox with 'Kit Fox (The Glue Factory)' painted on the front. And at the top of the fire escape was a heavy-duty metal door.

The Major led the way, tapping at the rickety steps with his walking stick before clambering up, the whole thing creaking and groaning like a ship being crushed by icebergs. Halfway up I stopped and looked out over the car park that was now a field of weeds. And parked in the far corner was a large white van and a green-and-white striped Citroën 2CV, with leopardskin seat covers. When we reached the top I saw there was a doorbell and a fancy intercom system.

'I thought this place was empty,' I said.

'Appearances can be deceptive,' replied the Major, pressing the buzzer.

Ten seconds later the intercom clicked on and a crackly voice said, 'Who is it?'

'Major Gregory and James Stoker. On a tiger hunt,' said the Major.

'Let yourselves in,' said the intercom.

And the door clicked open.

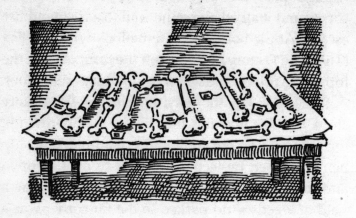

8

The Glue Factory

The first room was long and narrow and full of junk. A massive workbench stretched from one end to the other piled high with old tools, bits of driftwood, tin cans, rubber gloves and stacks of magazines. Hanging from hooks on the wall were three pairs of dirty overalls and two gas masks. Under the workbench there were dozens of cardboard boxes, covered in dust and tied up with string. The windows had cobwebs for curtains and the light was struggling to get through.

It was spooky. The whole place looked abandoned. As if whoever had worked there had left in a hurry. I was that busy looking at everything I kicked over a glass jar that had been left on the floor. Loads of what looked like dice rattled across the floorboards and crunched under my feet. When I bent down to pick them up, I saw they weren't dice, but *teeth*. I'd just finished scooping them back into the jar when I heard a click and saw the Major disappearing through the next door.

The second room was a bit bigger and wider. Instead of one long bench there were six smaller tables, covered in bones. They weren't scattered about, or dumped, like the junk in the first room. These bones had been carefully arranged, according to size and shape, on sheets of clean brown paper. The bones on the nearest table were the smallest. There were thousands of them; the smallest ones no bigger than matchsticks and the biggest about the size of pencils. After that they went up in size and down in number, from one table to the next, until the last table only had room for ten massive bones. The kind you'd expect to find cavemen gnawing on at the back of caves.

I picked up one of the smallest bones. It had a little white label attached with thin string, and on the label, in tiny, neat handwriting, someone had written, *Spider Monkey; Metacarpal; LO.*

I couldn't work it out. *Why all the bones?* And then I twigged. *Bones – glue – the Glue Factory –*

glue's made from bones. This must have been where they experimented with different types of bones, trying to make different glues. Maybe 'spider monkeys' metacarpals' were used for something really special, like sticking the little blue labels on bananas.

'Fascinating,' muttered the Major.

He was peering through the glass of a tall display cabinet. Inside were hundreds of tiny skulls. Birds mostly, but also rats and bats and things like that.

'Those remind me of the little ivory carvings you've got at the Manor. The ones you keep in your study,' I said.

'Ah, yes. The *netsuke*. The Japanese craftsmen carved them out of wood or ivory. They were used as toggles to fasten medicine boxes. I've also recently acquired some rather beautiful ivory seal charms, carved by Eskimos. Remind me to show you when you next drop by.'

'Did they use these bones to make glue?'

'An interesting hypothesis,' said the Major, smiling. 'But I suspect this wonderful collection has little to do with Mr Braine and his very excellent glue.'

At the end of the room were two doors. One was open and seemed to lead downstairs, the other was closed. The Major turned the handle and opened it. The third room was bigger and wider still; almost square. There were spotlights on the ceiling shining down on brilliant white walls and varnished floorboards the colour of golden syrup. It was totally empty, except for a five-bar gate propped up against the wall in the far corner. Perched on the gate were about a dozen rooks, their feathers glistening blue black. One of them was tugging at a piece of orange string, the kind that farmers use for tying up bales of straw. Some of the others were watching him. And some were watching us.

We both stood dead still in the doorway. Nothing moved. I kept expecting them to start flapping round the room, or at least shuffling about a bit, but they just kept staring in absolute silence.

'This is the gallery,' said the Major, 'where Kit shows the finished pieces.'

'Are they real?' I asked, still staring at the rooks.

'Dead as the proverbial door nail,' replied the Major.

Just then another door opened and a tall lady with short dark hair walked into the room. She was wearing a baggy black jumper, faded blue jeans and leopardskin slippers.

'Hi,' she said.

'Kit!' exclaimed the Major. 'May I introduce James Stoker? We were just admiring your rooks.'

'Good, aren't they?' she said.

'I thought they were real,' I said.

'That's the general idea,' said Kit. 'Do you want to come through for a cup of tea or something?'

'No. We won't keep you,' said the Major. 'We were rather hoping we might catch a glimpse of a certain Siberian tiger.'

'Boris?' said Kit. 'He's downstairs in the meat room, thawing out. I borrowed Mr Wong's van, like you suggested, and picked him up last night. I'll be measuring him later. And then skinning him tomorrow.'

'Are *you* the taxidermist?' I asked.

'No, I just like measuring tigers, then cutting them up,' she said. Then smiled. 'Yes. Kit Fox, Taxidermist. That's me. What did you expect? A man?'

'I suppose so,' I admitted, feeling embarrassed.

'Don't worry. Everyone does. It's my name. And the job. People don't expect a woman to be doing something quite so . . .'

'Gruesome?' suggested the Major.

'Bits of it are,' she agreed. 'But then, so's making a steak and kidney pudding. It all depends how you look at it. I just think of it as a means to an end. And if the end looks real, I've done a good job.'

Kit led us back the way we'd come, back to the first room with all the junk. Then we went through another door and down some other stairs to the ground floor meat room, which was a huge cavernous space with concrete pillars holding up the ceiling. It was cold and deathly quiet, except for the steady *plip, plip* of water dripping from a leaky tap. Most of the windows had been boarded up and it was dark, but I could make out certain things. Like two huge deep-freezes huddled against the wall and a table standing on its own in the middle. There was a dark shape slumped over the top of the table. I didn't need the lights to guess what the shape was. You could smell him in the cold, dark air. The whole ground floor stank of tiger.

'*Poo!*' said the Major, pinching his nose.

'He is a bit smelly,' said Kit, flicking a switch.

A single brilliant, overhead light glared down and the table burst into yellowy-orange flames.

Tyger! Tyger! burning bright
In the forests of the night
What immortal hand or eye
Could frame thy fearful symmetry?' recited the Major.

'Mine, I hope,' laughed Kit.

'Quite so. Quite so,' agreed the Major.

We all walked towards the table with our eyes fixed on Boris. Even dead, he was awesome.

'What do you measure?' I asked.

'Just about everything,' said Kit. 'I've got to be certain that when I put him back together he's exactly the same shape and size, otherwise the skin doesn't fit. I'll be doing a cast of his mouth later on. Do you know what I mean by a cast?'

'Yes. Me mam's an artist. She makes plaster models of animals. She makes them in clay first. Then she makes a rubber mould and casts loads of them in plaster. She does a great zebra.'

'I did a zebra once,' mused Kit.

'I am curious why you cast the mouth,' said the Major.

'He's going to be snarling. Showing his teeth. So you'll be able to see inside. Every little detail has to be accurate. Even the tongue.'

'Do you use his real tongue?' I asked.

'No. That's why I do the cast. His teeth and tongue and possibly his lips will be fibreglass. You can buy them ready made, but I prefer to do my own.'

'Ready-made tongues?'

'Oh yes. There's a whole drawerful upstairs. Everything from little forked jobs for snakes to walloping great cows' tongues. I don't know whether they do a tiger's. I expect they do. It'll be in the catalogue.'

It was time to go. Kit took us to the top of the fire escape.

'How's Monty?' she asked the Major.

'Still swimming,' he said.

76

Then she turned to me. 'I heard how you saved the Major's koi carp last year. Would you like to come back later and watch me work on Boris?'

'You bet!'

'Next Sunday then. Same time.'

9

Falsely Accused

On Monday morning Billy was waiting for me at the bottom of Church Street. He looked worried.

'Have y'seen Norman?' he asked.

'No. Why?'

'He ran off, five minutes ago, after this ginger cat. It was massive. Bigger than him. And he hasn't come back.'

'Which way did he go?'

'Up towards your house. That's why I'm asking. He's never done this before.'

'*Never chased a cat?*'

'No. Pillock. He's chased every cat in Larkstoke.

"Stormin' Norman" they call him. But he always comes straight back. He's never not walked all the way to school.'

'Should we wait a bit?' I suggested.

'Better had,' said Billy, resignedly.

We stood on the corner. Billy looking one way and me looking the other. But there was no sign of Norman.

'Sorry about Saturday,' said Billy. 'I should have phoned.'

'It would have helped. How was the shooting?'

'Great!' said Billy. Then, after a short silence, 'Well. It was all right. I mean, I didn't get to fire a gun or anything. There was my dad and six of his mates. They had the guns. I was just beating. You know, walking through the woods, making a noise, scaring the pheasants so's they'd fly out into the open and get shot.'

'Frank was a bit razzed off.'

'Frank's sorted. My dad gave him a couple of pheasants.'

We both looked back up the hill, but there was still no sign of Norman. It was five to nine, so we ran to school. When we got near the gates I saw Sam Warner and two others jumping about like they had ants in their pants.

'Billy! Billy!' shouted Sam.

'What's up?'

'They've got Norman!'

'*Who*'s got Norman?'

'The Wong sisters. They've captured him. I saw them both carry him into the Red Dragon.'

Billy opened his mouth, but no words came out.

'I'm sure there'll be some reason,' I said, trying to sound convincing.

'Norman's for the pot. *That*'s the reason,' sneered Sam.

'I'll . . . I'll . . .'

Billy was spitting feathers.

'You boys!' shouted Mr Ashley. 'Why aren't you in your classrooms?'

'Please, sir,' began Sam Warner, but his voice was drowned by the clatter of the school bell.

'Quick! Get along with you before I put you all in detention.'

We walked to the classrooms and sat down at our desks. Mrs Meredith did the register. When she came to Billy she had to call his name out twice.

'*William Gates? Are you with us?*'

But Billy wasn't with us. He was in the Red Dragon, smashing up the kitchens with a long meat cleaver.

'Here, miss,' muttered Billy.

'Pardon?'

'*Here, miss.*'

'That's better . . . Rebecca Holberton?'

After the register we all traipsed into Assembly on the lookout for Sheila and Sandra, but they were nowhere in sight.

'Told you,' whispered Sam.

Billy was white. He was sitting with his fists clenched and his eyes fixed on the row of seats where the twins should have been sitting. The violins started playing faster and faster and even Vivaldi sounded sinister. Suddenly there were footsteps behind us and Mr Ashley tapped Billy on the shoulder.

'See me in my office after assembly, William.'

Sam Warner lifted his chin and ran his index finger across his throat. He was enjoying this.

The rest of Assembly was a bit of a blur. Billy didn't come back into the classroom and we started lessons without him. At breaktime I went and stood by the school gates, trying to put as much distance between myself and Sam Warner as possible, but he found me.

'What d'y'think's happened?'

'I don't know,' I said.

'I'll bet the police caught the Chinkies chopping up Norman. I'll bet they're all in prison and Billy's gone to identify the bits.'

'Sam.'

'What?'

'Shut it.'

'I was just . . .'

But he didn't get much further. The words got stuck as he saw Billy walking towards the school gates with Sheila on one side and Sandra on the other. When they reached us the girls smiled and walked off towards their classroom.

'What're y'doing with *them*?' gawped Sam.

'What's it look like?' asked Billy.

'Did you find Norman?' I asked.

'He's got a broken leg,' said Billy.

'Told you,' smirked Sam. 'They must have caught the Chinkies just in time.'

'Norman was hit by a car,' said Billy. 'The driver didn't stop. Sheila and Sandra saw it happen. They carried Norman all the way back to the Red Dragon and their dad took him to the vet's. The vet said it was a nasty break and if he hadn't operated straightaway Norman might have lost his leg. Or worse.'

Sam was quiet. We all were.

Later that week I went after school with Billy to buy a thank-you card for the twins.

'I don't want nothing soppy,' said Billy.

'It doesn't need to be,' I said.

'I don't want anyone getting the wrong idea,' said Billy.

'Of course not. You're just saying "thank you".'

'That's right.'

'You need something simple, but appropriate.'

'Like what?'

'Like a dog on crutches with a bunch of flowers,' I said, laughing.

'Too soppy,' said Billy.

Eventually he settled for a card with a picture of a goalkeeper diving for a ball. Inside it said 'Happy Birthday' but he crossed it out and wrote 'Thanks for saving Norman'.

'D'y'think I should get them a present as well?' asked Billy.

'I would,' I said.

'My dad took four pheasants round to the Red Dragon last night. He said that's enough. But I think I'd like to give Sheila and Sandra something else. I mean, they might not like pheasant. And anyway, it doesn't seem right to give somebody something dead when you're trying to thank them for saving somebody's life.'

'No,' I agreed.

'What should I get them?'

'Flowers?' I suggested.

'Not flowers. I'm not walking round carrying *flowers*.'

'Chocolates then.'

'That's a good idea. D'y'think they like After Eights?'

'Almost everybody likes After Eights.'

'After Eights it is then. And Jimmy . . .'

'Yes?'

'Promise you won't tell anyone. Promise you'll keep it a secret.'

'I promise,' I said.

And then I remembered something.

'Billy, what was the secret you were going to tell me, that day in the school library?'

'Oh yeah, I nearly forgot. You know that woman that was making a tape recording of Olga roaring?'

'The one that Frank fancied?' I said.

'That's her. Well, she's one of them taxi-thingies. She's got Boris in The Old Glue Factory. And she's going to *stuff* him.'

'I know.'

'What?'

'I know.'

'Did Frank tell you?'

'No. It was Major Gregory. He knows the taxidermist. She's called Kit Fox. I've met her.'

Billy looked dejected.

'I was going to tell you,' I said. 'But what with Norman having his accident and everything, I just forgot.'

'That's OK,' said Billy, flatly.

'I'm supposed to be going back there on Sunday to see her. I'll ask if you can come too.'

'Would you?'

'Yes.'

'Promise?'

'Cross my heart and hope to die.'

'Great!'

10

An Ill Wind

Norman wasn't stormin' any more. He was confined to barracks with his right hind leg set in a splint. Word must have got round of Norman's incapacity, because the cats were coming out of the woodwork. Suddenly the back gardens of Larkstoke were bristling with bushy-tailed ginger toms; sleek blue-eyed Siamese; black cats; white cats; tortoiseshells and tabbies. There was even a rumour that the massive ginger cat that Norman had chased the day of his accident wasn't a cat at all but a lynx that had escaped from the zoo.

The hedgerows and tree tops echoed with shrill,

manic alarm calls. The birds were in a constant state of panic. The safest place for them was in the air. All the lawns were littered with feathered left-overs. All except the lawn in Billy's back garden, where Norman, 'The Bird Dog of Larkstoke', lay on the grass, chained to his kennel. Billy said the smaller birds, the sparrows and robins and things, would hop right up to him and sometimes even perch on his head. He didn't seem to mind one bit.

But if a marauding cat so much as poked a whisker over the fence Norman'd hurl himself, peg leg and all, to the end of his chain, snarling and gnashing like there was no tomorrow.

On Saturday Billy and I went to the zoo and afterwards we dropped the usual load of muck off at Albert's place.

'It's an ill wind,' said Albert when he heard about Norman. 'That'll explain it.'

'Explain what?' we asked.

'The sudden boom in the tiger poo business. Ah've been sellin' bags hand over fist this last week. I can't fill the flippin' things fast enough.'

We'd seen the new sign by the side of the road.

> **Don't be disapointed order now for Xmas**
> Put some Tiger Muck in yer stocking!

'There's this bloke I know,' continued Albert. 'City type. Snappy dresser, with one of those mobile phones. I met him a couple of years ago, when I was "on holiday" at Her Majesty's.'

'Where's that?' I asked.

'It's a big hotel up the road.'

'I've never heard of it.'

'Aye, and it's to be hoped you don't either,' said Albert, without elaborating on the reasons. 'Anyroads, as I was sayin', he dropped by yesterday for a natter and said I should get myself a website. Turns out it's nowt t'do with flies. It's all about selling things on the computer. It's the latest thing.

'He said that if my tiger muck was all it was cracked up to be I should be advertising it world-wide. He reckoned ah'd make a fortune. Imagine that. Albert Spark, on the computer, selling tiger muck *worldwide*.'

'Are y'going t'do it?' asked Billy.

'Ah'm giving it serious consideration,' said Albert, tugging at his beard. 'You've got t'keep one step ahead of the competition if y'want t'be top of the muck heap.'

'But y'haven't even got a computer,' said Billy.

'Not yet,' said Albert, 'but that feller I was tellin' you about reckons he knows where he can lay his hands on some, cheap. What you might call "factory surplus".'

'Sounds a bit dodgy to me,' said Billy.

'What's he want for them?'

'That's confidential information, young Master Gates. Let's just say I've come to an arrangement and I've t'find some brass sharpish. Which reminds me. Do either of you two know owt about stuffin' animals?'

'My dad does the turkey with sage and onion at Christmas,' said Billy.

'No. Y'daft barmpot. Ah'm not talking about sage and onion. Ah'm talking about *tigers* and the like.'

'You mean taxidermy,' I said.

'Aye. That's the word. Ah'm pleased one of you's got a bit of gumption.'

'There's this woman lives in The Old Glue Factory. *She*'s a taxidermist. She's stuffing Boris,' said Billy.

'What did you want to know?' I asked.

'I were just wondering about the bones,' he said, in a kind of distracted way. 'Once it's stuffed, she'll not be needing the bones, will she?'

'I don't know. Why?'

'No particular reason. But I might just pop on down to The Old Glue Factory, for a friendly natter like.'

'Me and Jimmy are going there tomorrow. Jimmy knows the woman who's doing the stuffing,' said Billy.

'Is that right?' said Albert. 'Well, in that case, you could save me a trip. Just ask her for me if she's doing owt with the bones. 'Cos if she's not, I'll give her a couple of quid for them.'

'What d'y'want the bones for?' asked Billy.

'Me arthritis,' said Albert.

11

Up in Smoke

Gran and Major Gregory didn't waste any time. The invitation cards for their birthday party were back from the printer's within a week.

Mrs Florence Stoker
and
Major Alexander James Alston Gregory
M.C. O.B.E.
request the pleasure of the company of
Mr and Mrs Gates & Master William Gates
at Old Manor House, Larkstoke, on Saturday
November 5th

7 pm till 11 pm

Chinese Banquet   Bonfire   Fireworks

'It's silly to waste money on stamps,' said Gran. 'You can deliver these two by hand.'

One was addressed to Billy and the other to Kit. So on Sunday morning, when Billy came round I handed him his card.

'It's their birthdays,' I explained. 'Gran's is on the 4th and the Major's is on the 6th, so they're having a joint Bonfire Night party.'

'What's it mean, "Chinese Banquet"?' asked Billy, running his finger over the embossed letters.

'The Red Dragon's doing the food. Sheila and Sandra'll be there and their dad's organized some spectacular Chinese fireworks. They're being brought up from London.'

'*Chinese* fireworks?'

'The Chinese *invented* fireworks.'

'I didn't know that.'

'You're coming, aren't you?'

'Of course I'm coming. Sounds great.'

'That's settled then.'

We set off up Larkstoke Hill. When we reached the top the Wychford Downs were shrouded in a haze of pale grey smoke, and orange flames crackled in the fields where the farmers were burning the stubble. Outside Albert's place there was a long line of parked cars. Business was brisk.

It was exactly half past eleven when we arrived outside The Old Glue Factory. It looked exactly the same as before, except this time there was a plume of black smoke rising from the tall chimney at the back, curling languidly through the yellow tree tops.

'It's all boarded up,' said Billy.

'That's just the front,' I said. 'Kit lives round the back and uses the rest for . . .'

'Stuffing dead animals,' interrupted Billy.

'Billy.'

'What?'

'You've got to promise not to say "stuffing".'

'Why?'

'Taxidermists don't like it.'

'Why? It's what they do. Isn't it?'

'Not exactly.'

'What are you on about?'

'I'm not sure. I just know the "s" word is banned.'

Jawohl, mein Kapitän. Vee vill not mention zee dreaded "s" word, joked Billy.

We were still laughing when we reached the top of the rickety fire escape and pressed the buzzer of the intercom.

'Who is it?' asked Kit.

'It's me, Jimmy. Jimmy'n'Billy.'

'Come in, "Jimmy'n'Billy". Go on down to the ground floor. I'll join you there in a minute.'

The door clicked open and we stepped inside.

'What a dump,' whispered Billy when he saw the first of the upstairs rooms with the long work-bench, piled high with junk.

'It's not all like this,' I whispered.

'Just as well. What's through there?'

'Bones. Millions of different bones.'

'Can I see?'

'Maybe later. We've got to go downstairs to the meat room.'

'The *meat room!* This is better than a Hammer horror film.'

We crept down the stairs like we were sneaking up on somebody. Every footstep echoing with horrible creaks and groans. Halfway down Billy grabbed my arm.

'What's that smell?'

'Tiger,' I said.

We carried on until we reached the meat room. Two cold, blue fluorescent strip lights glared down on the table in the centre. The table was bare. In the corner was a sink with a leaky tap that dripped, *plip, plip, plip,* echoing around the cavernous space.

'Where's Boris?' whispered Billy.

'The last time I saw him he was lying on that table,' I said.

'This place gives me the creeps. It's like that abandoned space station in *Alien*.'

'It is a bit,' I agreed.

'Where's the woman?' asked Billy.

'She said she'd be down in a minute.'

'It's been a minute,' said Billy, looking around nervously. 'What's in those?' he asked, pointing at the deep-freezes.

'Dunno,' I said, shrugging my shoulders.

'They're not big enough for a tiger,' said Billy.

'They're probably full of frozen food, like everyone else's.'

Billy walked over to the nearest deep-freeze.

'*D'y'dare me?*' he said, sliding his fingers underneath the lid.

'Go on then.'

He lifted the lid, slowly, and peered inside.

'What's there?' I asked.

'There's loads of bags, but they're all frosted over. There's pizzas ... Hang on! They're not pizzas. They're *snakes* that're coiled up like pizzas.'

I ran across to look. The snakes were wrapped round and round themselves in a circle, like Catherine wheels. Each in its own plastic freezer bag. The one I was looking at had alternate bands of white, orange and black. It might have been cheese and pepperoni, but it said '*Coral Snake – West Africa*' in black felt tip on the side of the freezer bag.

'You'd get a shock if y'stuck those in the microwave,' said Billy.

'What else is there?' I asked.

Billy reached inside and lifted out another bag. He breathed on the surface then rubbed it with his sleeve, so that there was a little window. Inside was a frozen hedgehog with its eyes closed.

'I suppose he's waiting to be . . . you know,' he said, putting the hedgehog carefully back where he'd found it.

'He's not waiting for the spring, that's for sure! What's that over there?' I said, pointing at a large dark shape that filled one corner of the deep-freeze.

Billy tapped it with his fist, then began dusting off the ice crystals.

'Something big,' he said. 'Something with ears and a long head. *Just* the head!'

'Hungry?' asked a voice behind us.

Billy dropped the lid with a crash and we both spun round.

'Don't look so guilty. I'm not going to tell you off. That's what you're here for – to look around. Right?'

'Sorry,' I said.

'Don't be. Come on through. I was disposing of Boris.'

'*Disposing?*'

'Well. Just the gory bit. It'd been lying around for a few days and it was beginning to pong. So I got the fire going and bunged it all in the furnace.

There can't be many people roasting tigers on a Sunday.'

'Was that the black smoke?' I asked.

'That was him.'

She turned the handle on a door in the back wall and held it open. Billy and I went through. It was a smaller room, right at the back of the ground floor. Outside you could see trees. Inside it was hot. The brick furnace was growling in the corner. On the left was a flight of stairs that must have led back up to the bone room and on the right, with just enough space to squeeze between the two, was a wall of tin cans, stacked floor to ceiling.

'Don't touch the tins,' warned Kit. 'Some of the lids aren't properly on and if they fall down we'll all be in a right mess. They're full of Braine's Best Impact Adhesive, guaranteed to stick anything to anything.'

We edged into the room, eyeing the wall of glue suspiciously. The first thing we noticed was the heads.

Round the top of the walls was a row of white plaster animal heads. There must have been nearly a hundred. There were foxes, deer, dogs, bears, cats, badgers, kangaroos, camels – *everything*. It was like a sculpture of Noah's Ark, with the animals sticking their heads out of windows.

'Wow! Look at that lot,' said Billy.

'That's my Rogues' Gallery,' said Kit. 'Do you like them?'

'You bet,' said Billy. 'Beats flying ducks, any day.'

'Did you make them all yourself?' I asked.

'Yes. They're all death masks.'

'*Death masks*,' echoed Billy.

'I always make a mould of the head and cast it in plaster before I start skinning an animal,' explained Kit. 'The head's what most people look at. And a death mask is the best way of ensuring it's accurate.'

'What's *that*?' asked Billy, pointing to a massive clay model with bits of real bone sticking out.

'*That* will be Boris,' said Kit.

'Are those his real bones?' asked Billy.

'Yes. I use his bones to support the clay model, the same way they support the muscles in real life. What I'm doing is rebuilding Boris's body with clay using all the different measurements I've taken, before and after skinning him.'

'How d'y'get the bones?' asked Billy.

'I cut away the meat,' said Kit, matter of factly.

'That must take ages,' I said.

'Ages and ages,' sighed Kit.

'Where's the skin?' asked Billy.

'It's being cured. It'll be ready in about a week.'

'Do you stretch the skin back over the clay?' I asked.

'No. The clay would need to be fired and it would weigh a ton. First I make a mould from the clay model and then I use the mould to cast Boris in something light and strong, like expanded polyurethane foam. That way I'll be able to pick him up and carry him upstairs. *Then* I stretch the skin back over and glue it in place.'

'So it's nothing t'do with . . .' began Billy, but stopped himself.

Kit smiled.

'Nothing,' she said, emphatically.

'And the bones in the clay. What's going to happen with them?'

'They'll become part of my collection. I've a whole room full upstairs.'

'So you're not throwing them out then?' said Billy.

'Not likely,' said Kit. 'They're much too valuable.'

'Where's Boris's head?' I asked, trying to change the subject.

'That goes on last,' said Kit. 'Would you like to see his death mask?'

'You bet!' we both said.

We walked across the room to a workbench, cluttered with bottles and tins and bags of plaster. In the centre was a huge blob of grey rubber.

'Peel it back,' said Kit.

I tucked my fingers under the base and carefully

lifted the cold, squidgy rubber up and over something hard. I was thinking about my mam casting her zebras, and now probably leopards and tigers and things. But this was different. This was the real thing. The rubber mould flopped back and we were staring at the ghostly white death mask of Boris the Siberian tiger.

'GGGGGGGGRAAAAAAAAAAAAAAAAGGG GGGGGHHHHHHHHH!'

A blood-freezing roar shattered the silence of the room into a million jagged pieces. Billy and I jumped out of our skins. Kit was laughing. I turned round and saw her click the button of a cassette player.

'Sorry. I couldn't resist it,' she said. 'That's why Major Gregory and I get on so well. We're both practical jokers.'

'Was . . . was that Boris?' stammered Billy.

'That was Olga,' said Kit. 'That's why I was at the zoo the other day. I wanted to record a real tiger's roar, to remind me what it is I'm trying to recreate. To remind me that, when those jaws bite, the teeth don't just cut through flesh. They cut through bone.'

Boris stared serenely from the workbench, his once cloudy grey eyes now pure white and strangely alert. His mouth was closed in the beginnings of a smile.

'I thought you were going to have him growling,' I said.

'I am,' said Kit. 'I did a separate cast of his mouth and I've found a ready-made tongue.'

'A *what*?' said Billy.

'Over there in the drawer. The one that says "Arghhhh!" on the front.'

'Why's it say that?' asked Billy.

'Take a look.'

Billy walked over and gingerly opened the drawer.

'Arghhhh!'

The drawer was full of tongues. There was a cow's, a wolf's, a horse's, two dogs', three snakes' and a tiger's. They were plastic, but looked totally real. All stretched out. Waiting for a mouth to call home.

'Would you boys like a cup of tea and a piece of cake?'

'I don't think I could eat anything right now,' said Billy, closing the tongue drawer. 'But I could murder a cup of tea.'

We all sat down and drank tea until it was time to go.

'I nearly forgot this,' I said, pulling the Major's invitation out of my coat pocket.

'A Chinese bonfire. Trust the Major,' laughed Kit.

'Are you coming?'

'I'd love to. Tell him I'll be there, just so long as I'm not behind with Boris.'

'How long will it take you?' I asked.

'A big animal like this usually takes well over a month. But I'm working overtime on this one as a special favour. I should have him ready by November 5th.'

'Who's he for?' asked Billy.

'Trevor Wainwright, the Director of Wychford Zoo,' said Kit. 'He's planning to auction the finished Boris at a big taxidermy sale in London in mid November.'

'Why's he want to sell him?' asked Billy.

'Trevor's not interested in dead animals. He's only concerned with live ones. He plans to use whatever money he makes to extend the tiger enclosure and buy a new mate for Olga.'

'Albert'll be pleased,' muttered Billy.

'Thanks very much for showing us everything,' I said. 'It's been amazing. No-one's going to believe it.'

'Yeah, thanks,' said Billy.

'It's a pleasure,' said Kit. 'I'll give you a call when Boris is ready to receive visitors, but drop by anytime. If I'm not working, I'll most likely be up there.' And she pointed to a door at the top of the stairs. 'That's where I live. Don't bother with the fire escape. Come round the back of the factory. There's a door that's hardly ever locked. You can't

102

really see it from outside because of the brambles. It leads straight out into the woods and there's a path through the woods back to the road.'

We said goodbye and left from the back door. The sun was already low in the sky, glowing a fiery orange between the tangle of trees. Yellow leaves were falling slowly and the plume of black smoke had dwindled to a wisp of grey.

For a while we walked in silence, each of us wrapped up in his own thoughts. Thoughts of tigers, and bones, and death masks, and tongues. Somewhere nearby a startled bird beat its wings and crashed through the branches in an eye-staring, ear-splitting panic. We turned to look. And as we turned we heard the roar.

Kit was playing Olga.

12

Albert Flips

Next Saturday we were back at the zoo and Frank was waiting for us. He was leaning against the snowy owl cage with his hands in his pockets.

'I want a word with you two,' he said.

'What's up . . . sir?,' asked Billy, nervously.

'Old Wainwright's found out about the tiger muck.'

'You mean, us taking it to Albert?'

'That's *exactly* what I mean.'

'Are we all in trouble?' I asked.

'*You're* in trouble,' he said, ominously. 'But it's nothing serious. Not if you keep your mouths shut.'

'How d'y'mean?' asked Billy, frowning.

'It's like this see, Wainwright doesn't know that I was involved. And I don't want him to find out. Have you got that?'

We both nodded.

'So, if you've got any sense, you'll keep your mouths shut about "Uncle Frank". Remember, it's "Uncle Frank" who does the hiring and firing round here. Do I make myself clear?'

'Yes, sir.'

'He wants to see you both. He's over by the tiger cage. Better make it snappy. And boys ... remember, this was all *your* idea.'

'We're in for it now,' said Billy, as we dragged ourselves towards the tiger enclosure.

'We were just doing what we were told,' I said. 'It wasn't us. It was Frank bloomin' Wiggins.'

'I know, but we took money for it,' said Billy.

He had a point.

Mr Wainwright was lowering the perspex cover over the Siberian tiger information board. He was a small man in a baggy, grey suit that looked at least two sizes too big for him. His hair had once been ginger, but that was mostly grey now too, and fell untidily over his eyes as he bent forward. His skin was pale, but his eyes were bright blue and sparkled with concentration. I realized immediately that I'd seen him walking round the zoo almost every day

I'd been there, but it never occurred to me that he was anyone important. He was always by himself, strolling distractedly from one enclosure to the other, pausing at each to talk to the occupants. He looked more like a visitor than the Director.

'Just a second,' he mumbled, taking two brass screws from between his lips. 'William, and . . . ?'

'James,' I said.

'Ah, yes. James,' said Mr Wainwright, putting the screws back in place. 'Did Mr Wiggins mention what it was I wanted to see you both about?'

'He said it was about the tiger muck.'

'Yes. I understand you've been supplying Mr Spark with tiger droppings for quite some time. Is that right?'

'Yes, sir,' mumbled Billy.

'Don't you think you ought to have asked my permission?'

We both hung our heads and stared at the ground. I was biting my lip, trying not to blurt out that it was Frank Wiggins who'd asked us to do it.

'I'd have been only too happy to give you permission. I'm delighted to see the tiger waste being put to good use.'

I lifted my head and looked at him. He wasn't angry at all, just slightly exasperated – the same way Albert had been, when he was rummaging through his rusty tin cans, searching for a bulb for the lamp on my bike.

'I don't know how you both expected to keep it a secret. After all, I could hardly have missed the signs by the roadside. And it doesn't take Sherlock Holmes to work out where the tiger waste is coming from.'

He paused and tapped the palm of his hand with the blade of the screwdriver.

'When I asked Mr Wiggins about the enterprising Mr Spark, he told me that he'd seen the pair of you, on several occasions, leaving the zoo premises with large plastic bags draped over your bicycles.'

Billy and I stared wide-eyed at each other. That rat, Frank Wiggins, had dropped us in it!

'And when I confronted Mr Spark he implied that a certain amount of cash had exchanged hands, although he didn't mention any names and remained vague about the precise amount.'

Good old Albert!

'What's going to happen to us?' asked Billy, meekly.

'Nothing,' said Mr Wainwright, tossing the screwdriver into the air and catching it in his other hand. 'We're all going to carry on as normal, except now it's official and above board. Mr Spark and I have come to an arrangement. We supply him with tiger waste in return for half the selling price, the money from which will be donated to the Save the Tiger Fund.'

I couldn't help smiling, thinking of Albert's new status as a benefactor of an endangered species.

'That's great,' said Billy, with obvious relief.

'I'm pleased you approve,' said Mr Wainwright.

'I'm really sorry,' I said.

'Let's put it all behind us,' said Mr Wainwright. 'I'm going to need all the help I can get round here. As you can see, I'm planning a rather special Christmas present for Olga.'

And he pointed at the information board.

Inside there was a new notice about the proposed extension of the tiger enclosure and a photograph of a massive Siberian tiger. Underneath it said 'FROM RUSSIA WITH LOVE – IVAN'.

'Magnificent, isn't he?' said Mr Wainwright.

'Awesome,' said Billy.

'Is Ivan coming here? I asked.

'If all goes to plan he'll be arriving on December 21st.'

'Where's he now?'

'Moscow Zoo,' said Mr Wainwright. 'We'll have to keep them apart until Ivan is properly acclimatized. You can't rush these things. But I'm hopeful that, by the spring, the new enclosure will be the honeymoon suite. We may even see some tiger cubs at Wychford Zoo. Poor old Boris was past it. But he's still got his part to play.'

'You mean, having him mounted and then

selling him at the auction?' I said.

Mr Wainwright looked surprised. 'Well, I suppose it was never meant to be a secret. The cost of the new tiger enclosure is more than the zoo can afford. The bank are willing to lend us most of the money, but we're still a fair bit short. So I was rather hoping that Boris might "save our skins".'

'I see.'

'Now, I assume you both have jobs to do?'

'Yes, Mr Wainwright.'

'Off you go then.'

Billy and I sorted out the 'blood and guts' then went off to help feed the penguins. It was such a relief, not to be given the boot, that every job we did, even the mundane ones, like sweeping the dead leaves into piles and carting them off to the tip, was fun. Sheila and Sandra turned up unexpectedly after lunch and Mr Wainwright said we could show them round. Billy and I felt dead important.

At four o'clock, when we went to fetch our bikes, Frank Wiggins was waiting for us with three black plastic bags. He didn't look quite as cocky as usual.

'Everything all right, then?' he asked, sheepishly.

'Yes,' I said, thinking, no thanks to you!

'These are for Albert, and this is for you,' he said, handing over thirty quid. 'Mr Wainwright says you're to get an extra fiver each for waste disposal.'

I took the money and winked at Billy.

'What's in this one?' asked Billy, lifting up a plastic bag that, judging by its shape, had obviously been filled with something other than tiger muck.

'Just some old bones,' said Frank Wiggins, dismissively.

'Does Mr Wainwright know we're taking bones?' I asked.

'These bones are nothing to do with Mr Wainwright,' snapped Frank Wiggins. 'I bought them off the butcher with my own money. Do you want to see the receipt?'

'No,' I said, taking a step backwards.

'Good! Then get on with it. And Stoker . . . it's "sir" when you talk to me.'

'Yes . . . sir.'

We set off up the road, side by side, sharing the bag of bones between us. For a while we didn't talk. It was amazing how one miserable person could change your whole mood.

'It's Halloween tomorrow night,' I said, breaking the silence.

'Hm,' grunted Billy.

'Are you doing anything?'

'Naw. Halloween's stupid. It's just a lot of kids dressing up and trying to scare each other.'

'So you don't believe in ghosts?' I asked.

'Naw. Why? Do you?'

'No. I don't think so. I've never seen one.'

'Me neither. If I had . . . what's *that*?'

We both looked towards Albert's place and through the trees saw what looked like hundreds of orange beach balls stacked in a massive pyramid. Albert was up a ladder, placing the last one on the top.

'Careful, lads. Don't breathe! It's taken me the best part of this afternoon t'get these pumpkins to stay put.'

'Where did they come from?' I asked.

'A bloke I know sold me them cheap. I was going to flog them for Halloween.'

'But Halloween's tomorrow night.'

'I know,' said Albert, miserably. 'I forgot.'

'How can anyone forget the date?' asked Billy.

Albert stared at him, blankly.

'You'll never sell all these.'

'I were going to say "Buy One, Get One Free",' said Albert hopefully.

'Even if you said "Buy One, Get SIX Free", you still wouldn't sell all of them,' said Billy, laughing.

'Happen you're right,' sighed Albert. 'That's why I've switched to Plan B.'

'What's that?'

'Signs are over there,' said Albert, nodding in the direction of the nearest shed.

There were two new signs:

> # BUY SoME MUCK AND SAVE A TIGER

> ## GES HoW MANY PUMPKINS AND WIN A CoMPUTER!
> ### 50p a shot
> ### Harf the money to TIGER ADE

'*Tiger ade?*' said Billy. 'Sounds like a fizzy drink.'

'Y'know what I mean,' retorted Albert. 'If you've got nowt better to do than make fun of my spellin' you can . . .'

'Sorry, Albert,' said Billy.

But Albert wasn't listening. He was clenching his fists and shaking his head, like a terrier with a rat's neck between its teeth. It was scary.

'Y'think it's a joke, don't you?' he snarled.

'No,' said Billy, plaintively.

'You do. You all do. Y'think Albert Spark's "touched", off his flippin' rocker.'

'We don't,' I said.

'Well, how do y'think it is livin' here? Scrattin' around to make ends meet. Ah'm at me wits end.'

'If you need money, I've fifteen quid,' I said.

'Me too,' said Billy, pulling his wages out of his pocket. 'That makes thirty.'

'Nay, lads, thirty quid's not going to get me out of trouble. You keep your money. You've earned it fair and square. Thanks, anyway,'

Albert had calmed down a bit.

'Is it 'cos you've got to give half the muck money to the zoo?' I asked cautiously.

'No. That makes no difference. I were giving half to Frank anyway. It's him that's lost out.'

'The muck's over there,' mumbled Billy, kicking at a stone that was stuck in the mud.

'And there's a bag of bones,' I added.

'Aye. The bones. There's always the bones,' he said, squinting thoughtfully at the third bag.

We left Albert, sitting on a pumpkin with his head in his hands, and set off up the hill. It started raining, that really fine rain that doesn't seem to go anywhere, just hangs in the air, soaking everything. The water was running down my face, and I kept on having to sniff it up my nose and spit it out my mouth. But I wasn't worried about getting wet. I was worried about Albert. We both were. We'd never seen him like that before. If he wasn't exactly 'happy' before, at least he'd always seemed in control. But this was different. Maybe he had too many fingers in too many pies. Maybe it was those "factory surplus" computers, or maybe it was the bones? What was he doing with a bag of old bones?

The mind boggled.

13

The Delivery Boys

It was Gran's birthday on the Friday, but she wasn't letting on which one.

'Life begins at forty, Gran,' joked Dad.

'Then it began a while ago,' said Gran.

'Happy birthday, Gran,' said Mam, giving her a kiss.

'Happy birthday,' I said, handing over a parcel that I'd wrapped in some of Mam's green tissue paper.

'What's this?' said Gran, acting all surprised and jiggling it about. 'It's quite heavy. And it's not soft like something knitted. But it's not hard like a box.'

115

'Come on, Gran! Open it!' we all shouted.

Gran placed it back on the kitchen table and undid the pink ribbon, which she wound neatly round her left index finger and slipped into her pocket.

'Waste not, want not,' she said, revelling in our impatience.

Then she began painstakingly to separate the sheets of green tissue, as if she was trying to do it without them rustling. It was like watching someone dismantle a bomb. Slowly the layers peeled away, until the white plastic shone through the green. Gran removed the final layer and read the message, scrawled in black felt-tip pen, on the front of the bag: SPARKS TIGER MUCK – *Guaranteed 100 persent PURRe!*

'Well ... I ... I'm speechless,' stammered Gran.

'I thought you could use it in the garden,' I said, 'to keep the cats off your tulips next spring.'

'How very thoughtful. It's quite the *nicest* present anyone has ever given me.'

And she gave me a kiss, then we all started laughing.

'Has it got a "use by" date?' asked Gran.

The zoo was closed on Saturday. The builders had started work on the extension to the tiger enclosure and Mr Wainwright didn't like the idea of diggers and dumper trucks driving round the place when it was full of visitors. It was probably just as well because, with the party at the Manor, there were a million and one jobs to do.

Dad and I set off straight after breakfast. It was a perfect autumn morning, as sharp and bright as the blade on a new penknife. The last yellow leaves were tumbling playfully through a brilliant blue sky and the bottom of the village was drowned in a slowly moving seat of mist. Roof tops, like battleships, floated on the surface, ribbons of grey smoke unfurling from their turrets. It looked like someone's dream – a dream we were walking into.

The path by the Manor House wall was littered with apples that no-one seemed interested in, except the wasps. I guess people preferred the ones in the shops that came from far-flung places like Chile. Our back kitchen was 'windfall city'. You daren't stick your head through the door for fear of starting an apple avalanche. Gran was doing her bit for global economy. She was making apple chutney. I gave an apple a kick and then Dad took over and we got it as far as the door in the wall before it rolled into the stream with a 'plop'.

Billy and the Major were waiting for us inside and after a cup of tea we started stacking the dead wood to make a bonfire. That took most of the morning and by the time we'd finished the top was covered in cloud – well, not *really*! But the sky was. A cold north wind had started blowing and the only blue left was the stormy dark blue of big bruiser clouds.

'Pity about that,' said Dad, frowning at the sky.

'It's traditional,' said Billy stoically, 'it always rains on Bonfire Night.'

'Maybe it'll blow over,' I said.

But as the words left my mouth a cold gust of wind swept across the lawn, rattling the dead branches, and doing its best to demolish out morning's work.

Billy went home to help his dad with something. We'd arranged to meet at five o'clock outside the Red Dragon, so that we could ride back to the Manor with Sheila and Sandra.

At five to five I skidded to a stop outside the Red Dragon and leant my bike against the wall. There was a small black van parked by the side of the road with a golden dragon painted on the side. The wind was still blowing and it was almost dark. Every now and then a solitary rocket screeched up into the sky and exploded in a shower of sparks. I pushed my hands deep into my pockets and for something to do started reading the illuminated menu, looking for Bird's Nest Soup or One

Hundred Year Old Eggs. But the weirdest thing I could find was Wind-Dried Duck. There was a squeal of brakes behind me and I turned round expecting to see Billy.

'Yo! Jimbo!'

It was Sam Warner doing a wheely on his new mountain bike.

'You should have your lights on, Sam.'

'Don't need 'em. Are y'going to the bonner at the playing fields?'

'No. I'm going with Billy to the Manor. I told you before.'

'What's wrong with the playing fields?'

'Nothing. But it's me gran's birthday. And the Major's. It's a kind of party.'

Sam looked kind of dejected and I started to feel a bit sorry for him.

'Is it right that Sheila and Sandra Wong are going as well?' he said, perking up.

'That's right.'

'Two *wongs* don't make a *right*,' he said, laughing at his own joke. 'D'y'get it? Two Wongs.'

'Yeah, I get it, Sam. Very funny.'

'And are you going to be eating Chinkie food? *Flied Lice* and stuff like that.'

'We're eating *Chinese* food.'

'What's the difference?'

'One's polite and the other's moronic.'

'*Oooooooo, sorreeee.* I forgot, you and Billy are sweet on the twins.'

'You can tell him yourself if you like. He'll be here in a second.'

'Naw. Can't wait. My dad's doing the fireworks and I'm helping. We've got fifty giant rockets and loads of bangers. See you.'

Sam disappeared and Billy arrived on his bike a couple of minutes later.

'Sorry I'm a bit late. I had to sort out Norman. He goes berserk when the fireworks start, so we keep him locked up inside.'

'Does he mind?'

'No. He thinks it's great. I got him *The Aristocats* on video. When I left he was sitting with his nose about two inches from the screen, growling at the telly.'

'Should we go in?' I asked.

'Suppose so.'

The notice in the window said closed, but the door was open. Inside, the Red Dragon was RED – red carpet, red walls, red ceiling, red chairs. The tablecloths were white, but there were red napkins and bunches of red carnations on each table. The place was deserted, except for a table in the corner, where two young men sat eating with chopsticks. They were both Chinese.

'Someone'll come soon,' I said.

Billy and I stood side by side and looked round.

There were strange smells in the air, strange and exciting. They must have been coming from the kitchen. On the wall facing us were two paintings in gold frames. One was of a dragon and the other was of a tiger. They were both painted on black velvet and the colours really jumped out at you, like someone shining a torch in the dark.

'They're good,' whispered Billy, staring at the paintings. 'You can tell they're good 'cos the eyes follow you round the room. We've got a painting at home like that. It's of this lady. I think she might be Chinese, except she's got green skin. *Her* eyes follow you. Even when you're not in the same room.'

I just nodded, staring into the beady eyes of the tiger.

'My ears are burning,' said Billy.

'Gran says that means somebody's talking about you.'

'No. It's all this red.'

'How come?' I asked.

'Red makes your heart beat faster and the blood rushes into your ears. I read about it in one of my mam's magazines. It's supposed to make you feel hungry as well. That's why they always paint restaurants red.'

'Fascinating,' I muttered.

'There's a gong over there,' said Billy. 'D'y'think we should . . .'

'Dare you!' I said.

'I dare you!' retorted Billy.

I walked over to the gong. It was about the size of a dustbin lid and made out of polished copper with Chinese writing stamped into it. The soft-headed drumstick hung on the stand beside it. I picked it up and gently tapped the centre, not expecting the wave of noise that suddenly flooded the room. The two men in the corner looked up angrily from their meal. A door behind us opened, and in stepped Sheila and Sandra.

'We are the genies of the lamp,' said Sheila. 'What is your wish, oh Master?'

'Sorry,' I said, feeling myself start to blush.

'*Sorry*'s not much of a wish,' laughed Sandra.

There was a clatter of plates and the men, who'd finished their meal, pushed their chairs to one side and sauntered towards us. One of them had a bleached, white stripe down the middle of his short, black hair, and the other had three silver rings piercing his left eyebrow. The smiles on the girls' faces vanished. The one with the stripe took a cigarette out of his mouth and blew a cloud of smoke over our heads.

'We're going now,' he said, letting the lighted cigarette fall from his hand onto the carpet.

He was just about to step on it when Sheila bent down and picked it up. She walked to the nearest table, holding it at arm's length between her finger and thumb, and dropped it in an ashtray. The smoker laughed derisively, then turned to his friend and nodded towards the door. They both left.

'Who were they?' asked Billy, following them out the door with eyes as wide as saucers.

'They brought the fireworks up from London. They think that just because they live in Chinatown they can behave like gangsters. In fact, they're nothing more than delivery boys.'

'I'm glad they're not delivering our groceries,' muttered Billy.

'What about the carpet?' I said, staring at a small black burn mark left by the cigarette.

'It doesn't matter,' said Sandra. 'Listen! We've something important to tell you.'

'The Bird's Nest Soup's off,' joked Billy.

'This is serious,' said Sheila. 'Someone came to see our dad today. Someone from the Zoo.'

'Go on,' I said.

'They had a bag with them. They said it was full of tiger bones. The bones from the tiger that died.'

'Boris?' said Billy.

'Did you see this person?' I asked.

'No. We were out shopping with Mum. Dad said it was a man.'

'Did he have a beard?'

'He didn't say. He just said the man was trying to sell the tiger bones.'

'What did your dad say?' asked Billy.

'Dad told him he wasn't interested,' said Sandra, 'but as the man was leaving those two yobbos from London arrived with the fireworks and Dad said that he saw them talking.'

'It's Albert,' said Billy.

'Who's Albert?' asked the twins.

'A friend,' I said.

'*You have friends that sell tiger bones?*' said Sheila, in disbelief.

'Apparently,' I replied, feeling very confused.

'There's something that doesn't make sense,' said Billy. 'How can Albert have Boris's bones, when they're stuck in a clay model in The Glue Factory?'

'They're not Boris's bones,' I said. 'They're not even tiger bones. They're just those ordinary old bones we carted up to his place the Saturday before last.'

'What?' exclaimed Billy. 'You mean he's trying to palm cow bones off as tiger bones?'

'Cow, horse, sheep, whatever. You've got to admit, this sounds like just the kind of stunt he'd pull.'

'If this is true,' said Sheila, 'your friend is in serious trouble.'

'You're not going to tell the police, are you?' said Billy.

'I wasn't thinking of the police. I was thinking of those two yobbos from London. Sandra and I heard them talking at the table. They were talking in Chinese and thought we couldn't understand.'

She sneaked a look at Sandra and smiled knowingly.

'They were saying how, if the bones were the real thing, they'd offer your "friend" a thousand pounds cash.'

'A thousand pounds!' gasped Billy.

'They'd be worth a lot more, if they were real.'

'But they're not,' I said.

'Exactly. And those two might be yobbos, but they're not completely stupid. When they find out Albert Whatshisname's trying to diddle them, it'll be *his* bones that are left in the bag!'

'When are they seeing him?'

'Now.'

'*Now?*'

'They said they were going to meet him as soon as they left here.'

'Oh no!' moaned Billy.

'Maybe we *should* call the police,' suggested Sandra.

'They'd throw the book at him,' said Billy.

'Perhaps he deserves it,' said Sheila.

'Perhaps . . . and perhaps not,' I said.

'What're we going to do?' asked Billy.

'We've got to get over there as fast as we can. Maybe we can scare them off.'

'You'll not scare off those two that easily. At least, not on your own,' said Sheila, glancing sideways at Sandra.

'And, besides,' said Sandra, 'you may need an interpreter.'

14

The Tower of Dragons

It was now pitch black and even though it was too early for the bigger bonfires to have been lit, you could see clouds of orange sparks climbing into the air from the smaller bonfires in people's back gardens. The wind was still blowing from the north, so it was on our backs, pushing us up Larkstoke Hill. No-one spoke.

By the time I reached the top I was completely knackered. I cruised to a stop and stood with my legs astride my bike, panting from the effort. I knew Billy was close behind and I expected the twins were some way behind him, on Larkstoke

Hill. But when I turned round I saw three lights bearing down on me. There was a scrunch of grit and everyone pulled onto the side of the road.

I'd never been on top of the Downs at night. It was kind of spooky. I knew there was this great view with rolling hills and fields and woods and the rooftops of Larkstoke, but you couldn't see a thing. You just sensed it was all there. In its place was a swarm of lights, pin-pricking the darkness like some mad dot-to-dot drawing without the numbers. Without any clues.

The yellow dots were windows where people hadn't bothered to close their curtains. And the orange dots were the smaller bonfires that smudged the blackness with trails of sparks and smoke. Every now and then another rocket would *whoosh* up into the sky and explode in a ball of coloured lights. It was a bit like the black velvet paintings in the Red Dragon, except here, there were no eyes to watch you and follow you round the room.

'Is it much further?' asked Sandra.

'No. It's just before the zoo. It's all downhill now.'

'Down into the darkness,' murmured Sheila.

And she was right. In front of us, there wasn't so much as a single spark. I'd half expected the zoo to be all lit up, but I couldn't even see it. It was the kind of black you get at the bottom of a deep well. The kind of black that can hide almost anything.

'I'll go first,' I said.

The wind was coming at us from the side now and we had to lean into it, or be pushed over. As we drew near Albert's place the clouds parted briefly and the moon peered down, turning the road into a ribbon of silver light. I slowed right down and switched my headlamp off. The others did the same. I hadn't said anything about keeping quiet. There was no need. Everyone just knew. I was looking for the black van with the gold dragon painted on the bonnet, but the road was empty and so was the driveway into Albert's. There was just his daft signs, nestling in the darkness by the side of the road and the jumbled silhouette of the junk yard.

As silently as possible we climbed off our bikes and leant them against the hedge.

'D'y'think they're here?' whispered Billy.

'I don't know. I can't see their van.'

'Maybe we're too late. Maybe they've kidnapped him and taken him to London.'

'Maybe,' I said. 'Or maybe they've just hidden the van somewhere.'

'We should go inside and look around,' said Sheila.

We crept into Albert's, sticking close together, trying not to trip over the junk that was scattered everywhere. The pumpkin pyramid was still standing, bathed in moonlight, looking like huge balls of gold.

'It all looks different in the dark,' whispered Billy. 'Emptier. Like there's something missing.'

'Let's hope it's not Albert,' I muttered.

'What's that?' gasped Sandra, grabbing my arm with one hand and pointing to the naked woman in the bath with the other.

'It's a mannequin. A shop-window dummy. It's meant to be a joke.'

Sandra let go of my arm. She wasn't laughing.

'If he's here he'll be in one of those,' said Billy, pointing at two old railway carriages.

'It's like a ghost train,' whispered Sheila.

'It *is* a ghost train,' muttered Sandra.

'They're quite cosy inside,' whispered Billy. 'The one nearest is what he calls his office and the other's—'

'*Look!*' gasped Sheila.

'Where?'

'The nearest carriage. There was a flash of blue light from somewhere inside.'

'Are you sure?'

'Positive.'

We crept closer. We could all see it now. It kept flickering off and on from behind one of the curtains. And there were muffled sounds, like someone trying to talk with a gag in his mouth.

'AAAAAAARRRRRRRGGGGGGGHHHHH!'

We all jumped back and dived behind one of the wrecked cars.

'W ... W ... What was that?' asked Sandra nervously.

'It's Albert,' panted Billy. 'They must have got him.'

'AAAAAAAARRRRRGGGGGGGHHHHH!'

We all shrunk back even further.

'They must be torturing him,' whined Billy. 'They'll be sticking matches under his fingernails and setting them alight. One by one.'

'AAAAAAARRRRGGGGHHHHHHHHHHH!'

'What're we going to do?' asked Sandra.

'I'm thinking!' I said, impatiently.

And as I was thinking Sheila bent down and picked up a half brick from the ground, and threw it at the door of the railway carriage. There was a massive *thud* as it bounced off, then the flashes of blue light stopped and all was deadly quiet. We crouched behind the wrecked car, watching the carriage door.

'Get ready to run,' whispered Sheila, as the door slowly opened.

'Hello?' said a voice.

'Albert?' I said, stepping cautiously out into the open.

'Jimmy?'

'Albert, are you all right?'

'I was until some daft barmpot started lobbin' bricks at me door. Was that you?'

'Yes. We thought . . . the screaming?'

'Y'daft barmpot. The screamin' was just the telly. Ah were watching an old horror film. *Curse of the Mummy's Tomb*.'

'I see. Sorry.'

'For heaven's sake. Y'can't go round lobbin' bricks at doors in middle of the night. Y'll give someone a heart attack. I thought I were done for. I thought it were the TV licence people. Are y'by yourself?'

'No. There's Billy, and Sheila, and Sandra,' I said, as they all stepped out of the shadows.

'Huh. A regular posse,' muttered Albert. 'Well, don't just stand there like a bunch of dummies. I suppose y'd better come in. Y'll have to forgive the mess. I wasn't expecting company.'

We all stood around like passengers on a platform waiting for a train, until Billy took the lead and followed Albert inside.

'Find yourselves a seat. Ah'll put the kettle on,' said Albert. 'And then y'can tell me to what, exactly, do I owe this honour?'

'We're here because of the tiger bones,' blurted out Sandra.

There was a long silence.

'Well, I'll be honest with you. When I heard about Chinese folks paying daft sums of money for tiger bones it did cross me mind that there might be a chance of making a bob or two.'

'But you couldn't get the tiger bones. Kit wouldn't sell them,' said Billy.

'No,' agreed Albert, looking more shame-faced than ever.

'So you thought you'd sell them cow bones and pretend they were tiger bones,' I said.

'I just thought bones were bones. Tiger bones, horse bones, cow bones. What's the difference? If you're going to grind them down and eat them, who's to know?'

There was another long silence.

'I'm really sorry,' he said, looking up at the twins. 'If I'd known the two of yous were friends with Jimmy and Billy here . . .'

'We don't *all* eat tigers,' said Sandra crossly.

'I know that,' said Albert. 'I wasn't thinking straight. All I saw was the money. I was being selfish and stupid. I wasn't even thinking about the tigers. But I am now. Mr Wainwright's lent me a load of books. Did you know that in the last fifty years *four* different types of tiger have become extinct? And there's less than . . .'

'But, Albert,' I interrupted, 'what happened to the bag of bones?'

'I sent them back to Frank.'

'When?'

'Last week. Why?'

'It's Frank,' said Billy, spilling his tea.

'You mean . . .' began Albert, suddenly realizing the significance of our visit. 'The sly beggar! We were going to split the money, fifty-fifty. It were all his idea in the first place. Then he got cold feet when Mr Wainwright rumbled the muck-running. And when I told him I'd changed my mind, he said it were probably just as well . . . But he must have gone down there on his tod.'

'Who is this Frank?' asked Sheila.

'He's the Head Keeper at the zoo.'

'Then that's where those yobbos are,' murmured Sandra.

'Have you got a phone?' I asked Albert.

'No. They cut me off last summer. What d'y'want a phone for anyroads?'

'To call the police.'

'*The police!*' exclaimed Albert.

'Frank's in real trouble. He's trying to sell the bones to two Chinese thugs from London. When they find out he's trying to trick them, they'll . . .'

'Pop his clogs,' muttered Albert.

'How far from the zoo are we?' asked Sheila, urgently.

'Half a mile, if that,' answered Billy.

134

'Spitting distance,' said Albert, kicking off his slippers and pulling on his wellies. 'You lot stay put. I'm going to see what's what. Frank Wiggins might be a snake, but I'll not see him chop-sueyed by any . . . Sorry, girls, I meant . . .'

'We're used to it,' said Sheila. 'But no-one's "staying put", Mr Spark. We're all coming with you.'

When we arrived at the zoo, led by Albert on an ancient rusty bicycle with no headlamp and no brakes, we felt as brave as an army. But any enthusiasm for rescuing Frank soon waned when we saw the black van parked outside the main gates.

They were here. They were somewhere inside.

'That's them, isn't it?' whispered Billy.

'Yes,' I whispered back.

'Are y'sure?' asked Albert.

'Positive. Look, there's the golden dragon painted on the bonnet.'

'Take the bikes and hide them round the corner. I'm just going to check that rear passenger side tyre,' said Albert.

We did as we were told and wheeled the bikes into the shadows as Albert got down on his hands and knees at the back of the van. There was a faint hissing sound and when we returned Albert was standing, with his hands on his hips, shaking his head slowly from side to side.

'Just as I thought. Flat as a pancake. They'll not get far on that.'

'When's your birthday, Mr Spark?' asked Sheila, smiling.

'What kind of question's that?' asked Albert.

'Quite a simple one.'

'It's April 1st, as it happens. And no wisecracks.'

'Aries,' said Sheila, triumphantly. 'I thought so. You're probably a dragon. You look like a dragon.'

Albert stared at her blankly.

'That's a compliment,' I added, hastily.

'Are we going in then?' asked Billy.

'Not so fast,' cautioned Albert, creeping up to the gates and placing his ear against the narrow gap, where they met in the middle. Everyone held their breath. The wind rustled in the branches of a large sycamore tree, and from somewhere a long way off we heard the faint rumbling of fireworks.

'Nowt,' whispered Albert. 'That means they're not in Frank's office. 'Cos that's t'other side of gates.'

'They must be further inside the zoo,' I said.

Albert tried the handle. The gates were locked and so was the smaller door to the side.

'That's a bit of a blow,' he muttered.

'That's it then,' said Billy. 'We're locked out. We'll never get in now.'

I looked up at the main gates. They must have

been at least four metres high.

'The main gates are padlocked,' said Albert. 'I can hear a chain rattlin' on t'other side. But that small door's not properly locked. Just bolted from inside. Is there no other way in?'

'Not that I know of,' said Billy. 'The whole zoo's surrounded with serious fencing. Barbed wire, the lot. The only other way in's to parachute in.'

'Ah've five army surplus parachutes in one of me sheds,' said Albert. 'Ahh'd a feeling they'd come in useful one day.'

Sheila's eyes narrowed till they were little more than fine lines drawn on her face. Albert smiled. 'Nay, lass. What we need's a ladder. Ah've half a dozen of them as well. But by the time we've finished fetchin' and carryin', Frank'll be history.'

Deep inside the zoo the silence was shattered by the spine-chilling screech of a bird of prey.

'We'll *make* a ladder,' said Sheila.

'What with?' asked Billy.

'We'll start with Mr Spark,' she said, smiling at Albert.

'Oh aye?'

'I'm going to climb onto your shoulders, but I'll need a hand up.'

'Are y'sure about this?' asked Albert.

'Trust me,' said Sheila.

Albert bent down, making a cradle with his big

hands so that she could step up and scramble onto his shoulders. Then, with a bit of a grunt he straightened his legs.

'She'll still not reach the top of the gates,' said Billy.

I didn't say anything. I just watched as Albert positioned himself with his back against the gates and Sheila, ever so slowly, stood up in balance. A sudden gust of wind shook the sycamore tree and Sheila lurched backwards. Albert grabbed her feet.

'Are you all right?' I asked.

'Yes. I'm fine.'

She looked down at Sandra and nodded. Sandra stepped forward.

'You're not . . .' said Billy.

'If Mr Spark's strong enough,' said Sandra.

'Don't worry about me, lass,' said Albert, making another cradle with his hands. 'Just so long as I don't have to bend down again. That might be a bit difficult.'

Sandra looked across at me and Billy and we figured out what she wanted. We each grabbed a leg and lifted her up so that she was standing in Albert's hands. From there she climbed onto his shoulders with Sheila so that they were facing each other. Albert's eyes were somewhere at the back of his head and I could see beads of sweat glistening on his forehead. The wind was still blowing, and in the wind you could hear the *pop-popping* of rockets as they exploded in the distance. It was like being at the circus. I kept on expecting to hear a roll of drums. Then, in one quick movement, Sheila cupped her hands and Sandra stepped up, mounting the top of the gates like a horse. She shuffled along to the end and disappeared over the side.

'What's happening?' asked Albert.

'Sandra's gone over the gate,' I said.

We all waited with bated breath until we heard the sound of someone jumping from a short distance onto the ground. The next second the bolt slide aside and the door swung upon. Sheila climbed down from Albert's shoulders and we all entered the zoo.

15

The Dangling Man

This wasn't the zoo that I knew – the daylight zoo, with its friendly hustle and bustle, its ice lollies and plaster zebras, its easy-to-read signs saying, 'This Way For . . .' This was the dark zoo. The zoo that only the animals knew. It felt dangerous, and not just because somewhere inside there was Frank Wiggins and two thugs. It felt dangerous like a jungle at night. That 'anything might happen' kind of dangerous, full of sudden rustling and scamper-ings, screeches and growls. You could smell the animals, and they could smell you.

The moon was behind the clouds. I kept thinking

we should have brought a torch, or at least a lamp from one of the bikes, but we were meant to be sneaking up on them and a torch would have been a dead give-away. I followed the edge of the path that skirted the picnic area. On the left I could just about make out the tables and chairs, and on the right were the desert foxes. They were shy, nervous animals with enormous ears, like furry satellite dishes, stuck on the top of their heads. They could hear a mouse sneeze half a mile away and must have heard us the minute we left Albert's place.

After a few minutes the path divided in two. Billy reckoned the Australian swans were to the right, but I thought they were to the left. It all looked different in the dark. I let Billy have his way and we followed the path to the right until we heard a huge splash.

'Big swans,' said Sheila.

'It's the sea-lions,' said Billy. 'They never sleep. They just keep swimming.'

'If it's the sea-lions, then the swans are definitely the other way,' I said.

We all turned round and I led the way back to where the paths met, then followed the left-hand fork until we came to a wire fence separating the path from a pond on the other side.

'I think they might be in here,' I whispered, crouching down next to the fence. Everyone else did the same. We could hear the wind in the trees, but not much else. Then, all of a sudden, there was a flash and a few seconds later a low rumble. At first I thought it was another firework, but then the drops of rain began falling. Slowly at first, in drops that you could count, *plip ... plip ... plip*, hitting the surface of the pond. There was a rustle of feathers, as somewhere in the blackness, the swans tucked their long necks under their wings.

'This is all we need,' moaned Billy. 'Some Bonner Night this is.'

There was another flash, quickly followed by a louder rumble.

'The dragons are fighting,' whispered Sheila.

'What's that?' I asked.

'In China, in the old days, people thought that thunderstorms were caused by dragons fighting in the sky. They would be afraid that the defeated dragons would fall down and crush their village.'

'It's "Stripy Head" and his pierced mate I'm worried about.'

'I don't think they're here,' said Sheila.

'So what do we do?' asked Sandra.

'Get out of this for a start,' said Albert, turning up the collar of his overalls as the rain began to fall with a vengeance.

'Let's keep moving,' I said.

The sound of the wind and the rain muffled our

footsteps and made us feel safer. I was in front, Sheila was right behind me; Billy, Sandra and Albert were a little way back. I'd been half walking, half running for nearly five minutes and I hadn't a clue where we were. On my left there was a short fence and behind that a tall chain link fence. I climbed over the short fence and pressed my face against the larger one. It was hard to make out anything in the dark, especially in the rain. One side of the fence looked exactly the same as the other. Sheila must have been thinking the same thing.

'It's hard to tell if we're inside or outside.'

'I'm pretty sure we're outside,' I said, as confidently as possible.

Just then there was an enormous explosion carried on the wind from a long way off. It wasn't thunder. You could just tell. It sounded like fifty giant rockets all going off at the same time. The whole zoo suddenly came alive with shrieks and hoots and growls. The animals were frightened and so were we. I could hear footsteps, running fast – *very* fast. They were getting louder and louder. I looked behind me.

'**GGGGGGGGGGGGGGGGRRRRRRRRRR AAAAAAAAAAAAAAAGGGGGGHH!**'

We both jumped out of our skins as a massive Canadian timber wolf hurled itself at the chain-link fence, snarling horribly with black lips curled back, baring nightmare yellow teeth. Then it was gone, as suddenly as it appeared. All that remained was the smell.

'You don't often see them that close,' I said, still trembling.

'That's a relief,' panted Sheila.

'What was that?' asked Billy, appearing out of the darkness.

'A wolf. It must have been scared by that explosion.'

'You should have had some mints handy. Wolves like mints.'

'I don't think this one was interested in mints,' said Sheila.

'Are y'all right?' asked Albert, bringing up the rear. 'It sounded like someone dropped a bomb on a jungle.'

'Fine,' I said. But before the word had left my mouth another roar, deeper and twenty times as frightening as the first, echoed through the trees.

'What was that?' gasped Albert.

'Olga,' I said, at the same time as Billy.

'Something's upsetting her,' I said.

'She's not the only one,' said Sandra.

'She's meant to be locked up in her sleeping quarters for the night.'

'GGGGGGGGGGGRRRRRRRRRRRRRRR

**RRRRRRAAAAAAAAAAAAAAAAAGGGGGGG
GGHHHHHHHHHHHHHHHHHH!'**

'She's not inside. She's outside,' said Billy.

'Dragons and tigers are sworn enemies,' said Sheila.

'Ah'll drink to that,' muttered Albert.

'They must be with the tiger,' said Sheila with absolute confidence.

'How do we get there?' asked Albert.

**'GGGGGGGGGGGRRRRRRRRRRRRRRRR
RRRRRRAAAAAAAAAAAAAAAAAGGGGGGG
GGHHHHHHHHHHHHHHHHHH!'**

'Follow the roars,' I said.

We all set off again, running through the rain, twisting and turning amongst the maze of paths. Pretty soon we were hopelessly lost. We could still hear Olga, but each time the roaring seemed to be coming from a completely different direction.

'This is useless,' said Albert, wiping the rain off his face. 'We're chasin' our own tails.'

'Let's get out of here,' said Billy.

'I would,' I said, 'but I'm not sure I could find the main gates.'

'I think they're back there,' said Billy, pointing over his shoulder.

'What about Frank?'

'Frank'll have to fend for himself.'

We all stood still. No-one wanted to make the

first move. The clouds parted slightly and through the branches of a tree I saw three bright stars in a straight line.

'Orion's Belt,' I said.

'What?'

'Those stars. It's Orion's Belt. Due south. If we follow them we'll end up at the tiger enclosure because that's at the south end of the zoo.'

Billy bit his lip. Albert scratched his head. The twins stared up at the sky.

'Come on then,' said Albert. 'Keep yer eyes on those stars.'

It worked. In less than five minutes we were all standing at the southernmost end of the zoo beside the tiger enclosure. The thunderstorm was still rumbling overhead, and the wind and the rain were lashing the trees, but there was no sign of Olga.

'D'y'think maybe she got out?' asked Billy.

'I hope not,' said Albert. 'What's all that over there?'

'It's scaffolding,' I said. 'They're building a new tiger house for the tiger that's coming from Moscow Zoo.'

'There's a light!' whispered Sheila, pointing at the base of the scaffolding.

'It's a torch,' said Billy. 'Maybe it's Frank.'

'Aye, and maybe it's his friends,' muttered Albert.

146

I opened my mouth to say something, but the air was suddenly split by a bone-rattling roar, so deep and awful that it seemed to be all round us at once. We froze on the spot as a flash of lightning lit up the flaming fur of Olga as she stalked through the long grass inside her enclosure.

'At least she's inside,' said Billy.

'What was that?' asked Sandra.

'At least—'

'No. There's another noise.'

'What did it sound like?'

'Like someone crying.'

And in amongst the wind and the rain we heard a muffled cry of help.

'*Charge!*' yelled Albert, running towards the scaffolding with his wellies flapping against his legs.

'*Charge!*' we all yelled, hot on his heels.

For a second or two the torch glared in our faces, then it turned and disappeared down a path. As we arrived at the base of the scaffolding we could hear the sound of running footsteps fading into the distance and the now unmistakable cries of help from above. Near the top were some planks forming a kind of platform and jutting out from the very top, over Olga's enclosure, was a long metal pole with something dangling from the end.

'Help me! Please, help me!' pleaded the voice.

'It's Frank,' I said.

'Not for long it isn't,' said Billy, taking a step backwards as the massive figure of Olga appeared with a low rumbling growl from the shadows.

'Look sharpish!' said Albert, as he set off up the scaffolding, arm over arm.

We followed behind him until we were all standing on top of the platform. Frank was dangling in the air about six feet in front of us, making whimpering noises. His wrists had been tied together and the belt from his trousers had been looped through and used to hang him from the end of the scaffolding pole, that was projecting over the tiger enclosure. His trousers had fallen down round his ankles and there were two lengths of rope tied to his feet. One trailed back to the platform we were standing on and the other hung directly down. At the end of it was a bag of bones suspended in the air.

'Ah've heard about being caught with yer pants down,' said Albert. 'But this is summat else.'

There was another heart-stopping roar from below and I looked down into the wild, staring eyes of Olga as the lightning flashed and the thunder boomed.

'She's frightened,' I said.

'*She's* frightened!' said Albert.

'She's hungry,' said Billy.

'Help me,' pleaded Frank. 'For God's sake. Help me. *Quick!*'

'*Pull!*' yelled Sheila, grabbing the rope on the platform that was attached to Frank's feet. We all pulled as Olga leapt and grabbed the bag of bones in her terrible jaws. There was a dreadful crunching sound as some of the bones cracked and splintered and the rest fell in a tangled white heap on the ground. Albert grabbed Frank's feet and hauled him towards us. The belt slid halfway along the pole then snapped. Frank fell backwards and downwards with his head and arms dangling above Olga. She left the bones and looked up.

'*Heave!*' shouted Frank. Olga leapt. Her massive paws must have been inches from Frank's head. You could smell the bones on her breath. Frank slumped onto the platform as Olga slunk back into the night, with a disgruntled growl.

'I thought I was a goner,' panted Frank.

'You nearly were,' said Sheila.

'Who's she?' said Frank, sounding really scared. '*She's one of them!*'

'Keep yer hair on,' said Albert. 'She's one of us. Here, give us yer hands.'

Frank held out his hands and Albert cut the rope with a penknife.

'You should be more careful about choosin' who t'do business with.'

'I never thought,' said Frank. 'I never thought they'd be able to tell the difference.'

'You don't need to be a genius to tell the difference between cow bones and tiger bones,' said Sandra.

'But I never thought they'd get that angry. I thought I'd be able to make a joke of it.'

'Some joke,' said Billy.

But Frank wasn't listening.

'They made me open her cage, then they brought me up here. They kept lowering me down with the bones tied round my feet until the tiger came. Then they'd pull me back in at the last minute. They were laughing.'

'Some folks have a funny sense of humour,' said Albert.

'I told them. I told them where the real bones were. But they just kept laughing and lowering me down.'

'What did you just say?' I said.

'I told them where the real bones were.'

'You told them about The Old Glue Factory?'

'Yes. It's what they wanted to know. They were going to kill me. They were going to feed me to that monster.'

'Did you tell them about Boris? Did you say Kit was a taxidermist?'

'No. I don't think so. I don't know. I don't care,' sobbed Frank.

'Is the phone in the office working?' I asked.

'No. They smashed it over my head,' moaned Frank, lifting his hand to touch a bruise on his temple.

'We'll have to warn Kit,' I said. 'She might still be there, at The Old Glue Factory.'

'How can we? They'll get there before us,' said Billy.

'We can go the back way. Take that path through the woods. Are you coming?'

Billy nodded, reluctantly.

'What about you, Albert?'

'Me . . . Ah've had enough adventurin' for one night. And I don't like this idea of you two chasin' after those other two,' he said, nodding in the direction of the main gates.

'We'll keep well out of their way. I just want to warn Kit. She'll have a telephone. We can call the police.'

'Aye, that's as maybe. And there's other folks'd say, "once bitten, twice shy". Is that right, Frank?'

Frank looked up but didn't say anything. His trousers were still round his ankles.

'Nay, lad. Ah'd best get Frank here back to base. He'll be needin' a stiff drink and a clean pair of trolleys before he faces the missus.'

I took one last look at Frank then started back down.

'I must be mad,' said Billy, clambering down the scaffolding. 'I thought the biggest adventure I was going to have tonight was going to be eatin' one of those pork dumpling things. And now I'm chasing folk that feed people to tigers.'

'We're coming too,' shouted Sheila.

I didn't argue. There wasn't time.

16

A Sticky End

We left the bikes by the side of the road, and started
down the path through the woods.

'Sssssh!' said Sheila. 'Listen!'

We all stood still as tree trunks. Over by the Old
Glue Factory we heard someone talking in
Chinese.

'What're they saying?' I whispered.

'One of them told the other one to get the axe,'
said Sheila.

'The axe!' gulped Billy.

'Not so loud!' I hissed. 'If we can hear them, they
can hear us.'

'The wind is from the east,' said Sheila. 'It carries their voices towards us.'

'Even so,' I said.

'Can you see anything?' asked Billy.

'Just their torch. There's too many branches in the way.'

'What d'you suppose they want the axe for?'

'My guess is they've found the front door, the one that's boarded up with planks and metal bars, and they're going to try and force it open.'

'Are there any other doors?' asked Sheila.

'Yes, there's one at the side of the building at the top of a fire escape. But it's a heavy-duty metal door – they'd never get through that. And then there's a secret door round the back. That's the one we're heading for. Kit said it's nearly always open.'

Somewhere in the darkness a van door slammed shut and half a minute later we heard the first THUD as the axe hit the front door. I reached into my pocket and pulled out my bike lamp.

'What about "Stripy Head"?' asked Sheila.

'They're busy. Let's risk it.'

I switched on the beam of the lamp and the path appeared in front of us, a yellow trail of sodden leaves snaking between the trees. On either side of it bare branches stretched out like grabbing hands. We began running, pushing aside the branches, tripping over roots, picking each other up and staggering on. Until finally we emerged into the moonlight at the back of The Old Glue Factory.

'There's a light on upstairs,' said Billy. 'D'y'think she's in?'

'I don't know. I can't see her car. What's the time?'

'Just after seven,' said Sandra.

'She's probably gone to the Manor,' said Sheila. 'The fireworks will be starting soon.'

'Great,' moaned Billy. 'Some Bonner Night. I'm scratched to bits and soaking wet. If I don't bleed to death, I'll probably die of pneumonia. Can we go home now?'

'Just wait. We haven't tried the back door yet.'

'What's the point? Kit's not here and there's two mad axemen bashing down the front door.'

'What about the bones?'

'Let them take the flippin' bones.'

'Then what about Boris? If those two find Boris they'll chuck him in the back of the van for sure. Then Mr Wainwright won't have a tiger to sell at auction and he'll have to send Ivan back to Moscow.'

'They don't even know Boris is inside,' said Billy. 'And besides, they'd never get him in the back of that van. He's too big.'

'They'll chop him up if they have to,' I said.

'What if they chop *us* up?'

'Then you can blame me. Or you can wait out here.'

'Let's try the door,' moaned Billy.

The door was open. I stepped inside and the others followed. It was pitch black. I swung the lamp from the right to the left, settling on the staircase and the wall of glue. Then I swung it back to the large table top, where the clay model built around Boris's bones had stood. It was gone. In its place were some massive plaster shapes, looking like giant bowls that had been smashed to bits.

'They must be the moulds,' I whispered. 'She must have cast him in bits and then stuck him together.'

'Where's he now?' whispered Sheila.

'I don't know. He'll be here somewhere.'

I walked over to the table and ran my fingers over the inside of one of the moulds. It was smooth as glass and wavy like the surface of the sea. The others were still standing just inside the doorway, looking up to where the walls met the ceiling.

'What are they?' asked Sheila nervously. I raised the lamp and lit up the rogues' gallery.

'Death masks,' said Billy. 'They're the heads of all the animals she's stuffed.'

'I don't like this place,' said Sandra, with real fear in her voice.

'They're just plaster,' I said, dragging the beam

along the line of heads. Watching as the foxes and deer and dogs and bears and beavers and badgers and camels and kangaroos all suddenly lit up, casting eerie shadows onto the ceiling. I followed them round the room, from wall to wall, until I came to the end of the line where the newest and whitest head stared down at us.

It was Boris.

'It's like a tomb,' whispered Sheila.

'*The curse of the mummy's tomb!*' said Billy, in a silly, spooky voice.

'She's right,' said Sandra. 'This place is full of ghosts – the ghosts of dead animals. I can feel them.'

'Where's the phone?' asked Billy.

'I don't think there is one down here,' I said. 'It's probably upstairs in the room above this one. That's where the light's on. That's where she lives.'

'I wouldn't live here if you paid me a million pounds,' said Sandra shuddering.

'Me neither,' said Billy. 'Y'see that furnace over there? That's where she burns—'

'Billy!'

'Wood,' said Billy.

'We should try the door at the top of the stairs,' said Sheila.

I crossed the floor and started up the stairs.

'Watch that wall of tins. They're all full of glue.'

'This is definitely the *weirdest* place I've ever been in,' said Sandra.

'Me too,' agreed Sheila.

We climbed the stairs and tried the door. It was locked.

'Can we go home now?' said Billy.

'There's another set of stairs at the other end of the building. From those we can maybe get into the bone room, and from there, maybe, into the gallery. And then, *maybe*, through into the room with the light on.'

'That's a lot of "maybes",' said Sandra.

'But it's worth a try,' I said, encouragingly.

'Hang on,' said Billy. 'The other end of the building's where those two loonies are. I'm not going there for all the bones in China.'

'You don't need to. I'll go by myself,' I said.

'We'll all go,' said Sheila with authority.

We ran back down the stairs, but slowed up when the wall of glue started rattling. Billy opened the other door and we entered the cold, cavernous space of the meat room, where I'd first seen Boris thawing out. The tap in the far corner was still leaking and the *plip . . . plip* of the drips seemed to fill the whole space.

'What's in those?' asked Sandra, pointing at the two deep freezes.

'Don't ask,' said Billy as a deafening THUD

echoed around the walls.

'It's "Stripy Head"!' said Sheila. 'He must be nearly through the door.'

THUD!

'Quick!' I said. 'Follow me.'

And I ran across the meat room towards the other staircase.

THUD! CRASH!

The door at the far end was splintering. I shone the lamp and saw the head of an axe, glinting like a silver tooth, before it was yanked back out, leaving a jagged black hole. We ran up the stairs, not worrying about the creaks and groans, through the long, narrow junk room and into the bone room. Downstairs another enormous crash signalled the end of the front door.

'Wait!' I said. 'Close the door and bolt it. Then push that table against it.'

Sandra closed the door, while Billy and I and Sheila pushed the table of small bones against the door. The table shuddered across the floorboards and the carefully labelled bones scattered and fell to the floor, crunching beneath our clumsy feet.

'*Oh no!*' exclaimed Sandra, stooping to pick them up.

'Leave them! There isn't time,' I said.

And we all ran the length of the bone room, flung open the door to the gallery, and stopped dead.

In the far corner the rooks were still perched on the five bar gate, but no-one noticed them. No-one was breathing. We were all staring at a fully grown Siberian tiger, whose eyes were glinting in the lamplight. I knew it was Boris. I knew he was dead. But my legs were like jelly as I waited for him to turn his head and roar.

'Is . . . Is that . . .?' stammered Sheila.

'Boris,' I said.

'That's amazing,' said Sandra.

'Awesome,' said Sheila. 'I can't believe he's not real.'

'I've had enough of tigers for one night,' muttered Billy. 'Let's find the phone.'

I walked across the gallery floor watching Boris out of the corner of my eye. From the side you could see he was standing on a large, low trolley with wheels, looking like some hideously over-grown child's toy. The light was shining from underneath the door to Kit's living room. I knew she wasn't in. She couldn't have not heard all the noise. I tried the handle. It was locked.

'Locked!' said Billy, despondently. 'That's it then. We're all going to be chopped to bits. And all because of stupid Frank Wiggins.'

There was another thud from below, followed by the sound of a door slamming.

'They're still downstairs,' I whispered.

'Maybe they've left,' whispered Sandra hopefully.

'Maybe our Norman doesn't like chasing cats,' said Billy sarcastically.

And, as if on cue, the door slammed again and we heard the sound of footsteps moving back through the meat room, towards the front of the building.

'They've searched downstairs,' said Sheila. 'They'll be coming up here next.'

'I'm getting out,' said Billy.

'There's four of us and two of them,' I said.

'They've got an axe. What've we got?'

I looked around. Apart from the rooks and Boris, the room was bare. There was only a black fuse box on the wall above the door and, over by the window, two cardboard boxes and a tape recorder, neatly stacked, one on top of each other. I looked at the tape recorder and then I looked at Boris on his trolley.

'What're y'thinking?' asked Billy.

I didn't answer him, but walked over to the tape recorder and, after making sure the volume was turned right down, pressed the PLAY button.

'Gggggggrrrrrraaaaaaarrrrrrrrrrrrrrrrrrggggggg gggghhhhhhh.'

I pressed STOP, then REWIND, and turned the volume back up to full.

'What're y'doing?' demanded Billy. 'Recording our Last Will and Testament?'

I lifted the tape recorder up and glanced down at the smaller box. On the top someone had written '*Assorted Eyes – Large*'. I lifted the lid and was met by the unblinking gaze of at least fifty glass eyeballs. I picked it up, listening to the sound they made as they rolled around. It was like water trickling into a still pool.

On the top, bigger box was written '*Siberian Tiger – Complete Skeleton*'.

'What's in there?' asked Sandra, pointing to the small box which was still in my hands.

'Eyes,' I said.

Sandra took a peek and jumped back.

'I don't believe I'm seeing this. I don't believe any of this is really happening. It's all too *weird*.'

Sheila came over, reached into the box, and lifted out one of the glass eyeballs. It had a large black pupil surrounded by a brilliant emerald green iris.

'It's beautiful,' she said. 'Beautiful, but useless.'

'I'm not so sure,' I murmured.

'Billy, take the lamp. See if you can open that door in the bone room. The one that leads downstairs. The one we tried but was locked. Sheila, fetch that box of eyeballs. And Sandra, see that mains switch above the door?'

'Yes.'

'If I give you a hand up, could you switch it off?'

There was a *click* and the light that had been seeping into the gallery from behind the locked door of the living room went out.

'Now the whole building's in darkness,' I said. 'They've only got a torch. Same as us.'

'It's open!' said Billy excitedly. 'I got it open. We can all escape out the back.'

'You three go. I'm staying. I've got a plan.'

'It'd better be a good 'un,' said Billy.

'We've switched out the lights in the building,' said Sandra.

'Is that it?' asked Billy incredulously. 'What're we going to do? Play chasey in the dark?'

'Here!' I said, passing Billy the box of glass eyeballs. 'Make yourself useful and scatter these at the top of the stairs.'

'Are you mad, or just stark raving bonkers?'

'No. He's *sly*, like a rat,' laughed Sheila, taking the box and doing the job.

'Give me a hand to move Boris,' I said. 'I want him back against the wall facing the door.'

'I don't like to touch him,' said Sandra.

'Then fetch the tape recorder. Billy and I'll deal with Boris.'

'The glass eyeball trap is set,' said Sheila. 'What now?'

'Shut the door and bolt it. Everyone behind Boris. When I give the signal, push like mad.'

'What's the signal?' asked Sandra.

'Don't worry. You won't miss it.'

I switched off the torch and we all crouched down in complete darkness behind the massive hind quarters of Boris. I know it sounds stupid, but somehow I felt safe, as if he was protecting us. Even so, my heart was thumping like a drum and all of us could hardly breathe for wondering when 'Stripy Head' and his mate would arrive.

We didn't have to wait long. The unbearable silence was broken by the ominous sound of the far door in the bone room rattling against its bolt. There were muffled voices, a few seconds of quiet, then a crash as the axe smashed the lock and the door banged against the table. More angry voices, followed by grunts and groans and the scraping of the table, spilling the remainder of the small bones onto the floor. Then quiet, broken only by small, crunching sounds and low voices.

'Can you hear what they're saying?' I whispered into Sheila's ear.

'They say it's a graveyard.'

'They say they've never seen so many bones.'

'They say the small ones are too small and the big ones are too big.'

'These are not tiger bones.'

'They think it is an evil place.'

'One of them wants to leave.'

The beam of their torch crept underneath the door.

The handle turned.

The bolt rattled.

Everyone took a deep breath and scrunched together behind Boris.

CRASH!

The door burst open and the beam of the torch fell on the snarling face of Boris, the Siberian tiger.

I pressed the PLAY button.

'**GGGGGGGGGGGGGGRRRRRRRRRRRRRRR RRRRRRRAAAAAAAAAAAAAAAAAAAAAAAG GGGGGGGGGGGGGGHHHHHHHHHHHHHHHH-HHHHHHHHHHHHHHHHHHHHH!**'

And Boris leapt forward towards the open door, the sound of his wheels being drowned by the tape recording of Olga's roar and the terrified screams of our assailants.

Boris crashed into a doorframe and came to a stop, but the two bully boys kept moving. They ran for the open door that led to the staircase, lost their footing on the glass eyeballs, and went head over heels down the stairs, landing at the bottom in a heap.

It was then that the creaking began, quietly at first, then louder, intermingled with the sound of sliding tins.

Then, '*AAAAAARRRRRGGGGGGHHHHHH!*', which didn't need any translation, as the wall of glue tumbled forward and crashed down on the heads of the hapless duo.

I leapt over Boris's shoulders, ran across to the open door and shone my lamp down into the black well of the staircase. It was a truly amazing sight. They were both completely buried beneath a mountain of tins, several of which had lost their lids and were oozing evil-looking, evil-smelling sludge. There was no movement, no sound, except for the *k-donk . . . k-donk . . . k-donk* of a single glass eyeball as it tumbled down the stairs.

For one awful moment I thought they might be dead, but then some of the tins began stirring and an arm, and then a leg, broke the sticky surface. I quietly closed the door and slid the bolt back across. Billy was right behind me clutching an enormous axe. The twins were behind Billy with their arms round each other's shoulders. And Boris was behind them.

'We've saved Boris!' said Billy.

'It's more like *he* saved *us*,' said Sandra, tentatively patting his head.

'Ssssssh!' I whispered.

The clatter of tins continued, mingled with curses in both Chinese and English. Then a door slammed shut and outside we heard the low grumbling of an engine starting up.

'What's that?' asked Sheila.

'I haven't got a clue,' I said. 'It can't be their van. That's round the front.'

The engine outside revved louder and in amongst the noise we heard, '*Charge!*'

We vaulted over Boris and ran across to the window in time to see the glue-covered gangsters frozen in the headlights of a massive digger. The digger lowered its bucket and drove straight at them. They started running. The digger stopped, turned, and drove after them, chasing them through the parking lot, out of the gate and onto the road.

We ran downstairs, clambering over the tins, trying not to stand in the spilt glue. By the time we arrived at the car park the digger had returned. The giant bucket was gently lowered, the engine fell silent and down onto the flattened willow herb jumped a big man wearing dirty red overalls and wellies.

'Albert!' shouted Sheila.

'Now, lass. That's how we deal with punks in Grimsby.'

'You *are* a dragon,' laughed Sandra, jumping up and kissing him on the cheek.

'Aye, well, if you say so,' said Albert, turning red beneath his bushy black beard. 'I dare say we'll not be seein' those two in a hurry. They've a long walk back to London.'

'What's happened to their van?' I asked.

'I shifted it for them,' said Albert, nodding back towards the digger. 'Parked it upside down in a ditch across the road.'

'You're mad!' said Billy.

'Mad and bad,' laughed Albert.

'Where did you get the digger?' asked Sheila.

'Borrowed it,' said Albert. 'By the way, did you phone the police?'

'No.'

'Just as well,' he muttered.

'It's a bit of a mess in there,' I said. 'We'll have to find Kit and tell her. We'll have to tell the police as well.'

'If y'must,' sighed Albert.

'How's Frank?' asked Billy.

'A gibberin' wreck. He says he'll never set foot in that zoo again. But he'll probably feel different on Monday morning. The fact is, the last thing he needs right now is the coppers breathin' down his neck. Yon tiger did enough of that. It'd be doin' him, and me, a kindness, if you were to keep tonight's antics to yourselves.'

'But we've got to explain the damage,' I protested.

'I realize that,' said Albert. 'But, maybes, y'could

be a bit "selective" with your explanations.'

'You mean not mention Frank and the bones, or you?' said Billy.

'Summat like that,' said Albert, scratching at his beard and looking pleadingly at the four faces in front of him.

I thought about Frank. I thought about having to call him 'sir'. I thought about how he'd dropped me and Billy in it with the tiger muck. But then I thought about him sitting on top of the scaffolding sobbing, with his trousers round his ankles.

'OK,' I said.

'OK,' said Billy.

Albert turned to the twins.

'Frank who?' said Sheila.

'That's the spirit,' said Albert. ' "The Four Musketeers". One for all and all for one!'

'Five,' said Sheila. 'You're one of us.'

17

Little White Lies

When we hadn't shown up at the Manor for the lighting of the bonfire Mr Wong and Dad had driven to the Red Dragon looking for us. When we weren't there, they had driven out to the playing fields to see if we'd called in at the village bonfire first. They had arrived at the same time as the fire brigade and stayed to watch them put it out. It was the north wind that was to blame. It had not long been lit when it started to get out of control. The sparks were flying everywhere and some of them landed in the box where Sam Warner's dad was storing the giant rockets. That was the explosion we heard in the zoo.

No-one was hurt, but someone called the fire brigade. And they weren't taking any chances. And by that time, everyone started to get worried about us and Major Gregory called the police.

The police met us at the top of Larkstoke Hill, so when we eventually showed up at the Manor it was with an escort. Needless to say, the party wasn't exactly the big celebration everyone had been expecting. In fact, it was a complete washout. The black circle of wet ash left by the dead bonfire said it all.

We'd all decided what we were going to say. And we all stuck to our story, for Albert's sake – and, I suppose, for Frank's as well. I'm not saying it was right. But it wasn't like we were lying. It was just that we didn't tell the whole truth. We simply said we'd gone out to The Old Glue Factory to look for Kit and stumbled upon the break-in.

As it happened, no-one asked any awkard questions. They all believed us. All, that is, except Gran. She didn't say anything, but I could tell she knew there was more to our story than we were letting on. It was a strange feeling. Because, on the one hand, we were the heroes that had reported the break-in. And, on the other, we were the villains that had ruined the party.

We left the Major standing over by the apple trees, poking at the bonfire with his walking stick.

The drive back home was awful. No-one spoke. I sat in the back with Gran. She kept her head turned away from me the whole time, staring out of the window into the blackness. I felt dreadful. Even the memory of Frank Wiggins with his pants down wasn't enough to lighten the burden of guilt that seemed to hang around my neck like a steel collar.

The next day things were slightly better and we all went round to The Old Glue Factory to help Kit put things straight. The police were already there, hauling a small black van with a gold dragon painted on the bonnet out of the ditch. There was glue all over the door handles and the rear passenger-side tyre was as flat as a pancake.

Dad and Mr Wong patched up all of Kit's dismembered doors, while Mam and Kit sorted out the bone room. Most of the small bones were smashed to bits on the floor, but they gathered up the ones that were still whole and laid them out neatly on the table top. It was no use labelling them, because no-one could tell the difference between a monkey's finger and a rat's hind leg. They all looked the same.

Me, Billy, the twins and the Major were put in charge of clearing up the mess at the bottom of the stairs. It was like photographs you see of places that have been bombed. We didn't know where to begin, but the Major took charge and we soon had all the tins outside stacked against the wall, like soldiers on parade. Luckily most of them still had their lids intact and there wasn't as much spilt glue as we'd thought.

Gran stayed at home.

I'd expected Kit to be upset, but she was just her normal self. She didn't seem to be bothered about the damage, the only thing that mattered was that her strange family of dead animals was all safe.

'There's something I don't understand,' she said, when the Major had gone upstairs. 'Why would anyone go to so much trouble to break in and then leave without taking anything?'

'Maybe they were after money and jewels,' suggested Billy. 'And when they found out there were just bones and dead animals they got mad and smashed the place up.'

'Possibly,' said Kit, in a tone of voice that suggested she thought it was anything *but* possible. 'And possibly *someone* scared them off?'

We all looked at each other and then back at Kit as she opened a cupboard and lifted out the tape recorder. She turned the volume up and then pressed the PLAY button.

At first there was just a lot of clattering, and then:

'We've saved Boris!'

'It's more like he saved us.'

'Sssssssh!'

'What's that?'

'I haven't got a clue. It can't be their van. That's round the front.'

'Charge . . .'

She switched it off and put the tape recorder back inside the cupboard. Someone had accidentally pressed the RECORD button just after the two would-be thieves had fallen down the stairs.

'I don't know how you did it,' said Kit. 'And I don't know why you did it. And I can't begin to imagine why it is you want to keep quiet about it . . . But thanks.'

At four o'clock when we'd finished we all sat round the big table in the studio, watched over by the rogues' gallery, and had tea with biscuits and little animals that Kit had made out of different coloured marzipan. Mam was right at home. When it was over the Major stood up and clinked his teacup with a spoon.

'Ladies and gentlemen, I have it on good authority that Master William Gates will be celebrating his birthday next Saturday. And by a happy coincidence, that is also the evening of the full moon . . . I have a question for you.'

We all looked at each other and then back at him, wondering what he was going to say next.

'Do you believe in dragons?'

Everyone said yes, even Mam and Dad.

'Excellent! I am sure you are all aware of the

174

significant role that dragons play in Chinese culture. I have just had a very interesting conversation with Mr Wong, in which he informed me that dragons are extremely fond of pearls They believe pearls to be droplets that fall like rain from the moon into the sea, which are then swallowed by oysters. They regard the moon as a giant pearl. In recognition of this there is a rather special festival, the Mid-Autumn Festival, to celebrate the beauty of the moon. It all sounds rather jolly. Although it is now *late* autumn, I propose that next Saturday we *all* meet at the Manor to celebrate *three* birthdays and the beauty of the moon.'

It was the best news. Everything seemed to be working out. Somehow, we'd all got away with it.

At least, that's what we thought.

18

First, The Good News

It was the biggest thing that had ever happened in Larkstoke. The Major didn't just invite us, he invited the entire village. November 5th had been a dead loss and everyone was grateful for a second chance to get together and see some fireworks. The place was buzzing.

On Saturday morning Billy took me by surprise and called for me half an hour earlier than usual. I'd only just got dressed and the Frosties were still in the packet. When I opened the back door he was standing there, hopping from one foot to the other, like the flagstones were red hot.

'Do you need the loo?' I asked.

'Have y'heard?' he asked, ignoring the question.

'Heard what?'

'The police have arrested Albert.'

I heard what he said, but I didn't want to believe it. The words seemed to wash over me, echoing down the passageway and finally fading into the silence of the empty kitchen.

'Come in,' I said quietly.

'Didn't you hear me?'

'Sit down.'

'*The police have arrested Albert!*' shouted Billy, slamming his fist down on the table and toppling the packet of Frosties.

'Quiet. You'll wake everyone up.'

'Sorry.'

'What did they arrest him for?'

'Possession of stolen goods.'

'What stolen goods?'

'Computers. My dad says he's had it this time. They'll throw the book at him 'cos of his record.'

'How did they catch him?'

'The police went round there on Monday to ask him about the break-in at The Old Glue Factory. It was just a routine enquiry. Did he see anything suspicious? That kind of thing. But when they were backing out they bumped into his pumpkin pyramid and knocked it over. All the pumpkins rolled away and underneath were six brand-new computers, packed in boxes.'

'Factory surplus,' I muttered.

'Factory "knock-offs" more like,' said Billy.

'What's going to happen to him?'

'Six months my dad reckons.'

It was like a cloud passing over the sun on a perfect day. I sat down beside Billy and scraped the spilt cereal back into the packet. The cartoon tiger was smiling.

'We'd best get going,' said Billy.

We took our time up Larkstoke Hill and cruised down the other side. I don't remember much about the ride, except that it was cold and the road was wet from the rain the night before. Albert's place looked desolate. Even the junk seemed to have shrunk down into the mud. The only sign of life was the naked woman in the bath, who still looked as fresh as ever. 'The Tiger Muck Emporium' had lost its Spark.

'What's that?' said Billy, pointing at a single solitary sign by the side of the road.

It said:

BILLY and JIMMY

Pinned to the top was an envelope in a see-through plastic bag. It was addressed to 'The 4 Musketeers'. And inside was a letter written on the back of an old electricity bill.

Dear Lads and Lasses,

I've to go away for a bit. A few weeks in Montycarlo at that hotel I were tellin you abowt. So I won't be at party Satterday night. But I didnt want to go not wishin Billy Hapy Birthday and all. Thers a world war 2 gas mask in a bag by the far shed that I thort Billy mite like. Itl come in useful if he ever has to muck out tigers. Watch out for draguns and stick to the strait and narra.

Best Wishes,

Albert.

Billy trudged over to the shed and returned carrying the bag containing the gas mask. In the aftermath of the 'bombshell' I'd completely forgotten it was Billy's birthday.

'Happy Birthday,' I said. 'Aren't you going to open it?'

'Naw. Maybe later,' he sniffed.

Frank Wiggins had been off all week with a 'mysterious illness'. The builders had packed up and left. And Mr Wainwright was wearing a new suit. He was standing in front of the tiger enclosure, surrounded by a disorderly scrum of local reporters.

'One more picture, Mr Wainwright.'

'That's it. Left a bit. Hand resting on the cage.'

'Head up.'

'Smile.'

Mr Wainwright lifted his head and caught our eye.

'How about one with my two stalwart helpers?' he suggested.

'Great.'

'Come over here, boys.'

We put the buckets we were carrying down on the path and sauntered over. The reporters and photographers stepped aside to let us through.

And then we saw him.

He was lying stretched out on a slab of rock, all four metres of him. He'd arrived from Moscow Zoo on Friday afternoon and was totally jet-lagged. But awesome.

We were speechless.

'Perhaps one either side of you?'

Billy stood on his left and I stood on his right. Mr Wainwright put his arms around our shoulders and we all smiled at the cameras. The reporters left and Mr Wainwright loosened the buttons of his jacket.

'It's all thanks to Boris,' he sighed.

'Did you . . .?'

'Indeed we did. The auction was a great success. Boris was bought by an Arabian sheikh for twice the amount we'd been expecting. Not only that, but the gentleman in question made a very generous donation to the zoo. In fact, there's enough left over to buy a couple of flamingos.'

'That'll keep the foxes happy,' whispered Billy. But luckily Mr Wainwright didn't hear.

19

Absent Dragons

This time we weren't taking any chances. Billy and I arrived at the Manor at six o'clock to find the garden totally transformed. The sky was that blue-black you get before it turns really dark. It was mostly clear except for a few lonely clouds drifting close to the horizon. The moon was hiding behind the wood, framing the tops of the trees in a halo of brighter blue and above the hills to the south, Orion's belt was stretched taut and straight like a diagram in some geometry book.

Dad and Major Gregory had hung lanterns from some of the trees and were going round lighting the candles inside. There was also a line of lanterns dangling from poles that were stuck in the grass, snaking across the lawn towards the pond. The arched footbridge and the little island twinkled with more lanterns that reflected in the black mirror of the water. Somewhere beneath the surface the Major's koi carp 'generals' were slowly swimming and probably wondering why the stars were closer than usual.

Over by the front of the house was the biggest table I'd ever seen. It must have been five or six all shoved together and covered with white table-cloths. It was waiting for the Chinese banquet that Mr and Mrs Wong had been preparing all day. We helped light the last of the lanterns and then Dad showed us the roped-off area where the fireworks were waiting to be set off. They were massive. Bigger than anything in the shops. There were square ones, round ones, short ones, tall ones – all with pictures of snakes and dragons, strange birds and Chinese writing, curling up the sides towards the blue black paper that was twisted to a point, waiting for a match to set them hissing into life. They all looked the business, but the most im-pressive by far was an enormous screen of bamboo poles, which supported a whole wall of fireworks tied together with a spaghetti of blue string.

'What's that?' asked Billy.

'That's the grand finale,' said Dad. 'You'll find out later tonight.'

There was a scrunch of gravel and we turned to see Mr Wong's van at the end of the drive. We both started running across the lawn to meet Sheila and Sandra. At least, we ran halfway and then slowed to a walk, remembering that we had to break the news about Albert. I felt like I imagined the firemen must have felt when they arrived to put out the village bonfire. It was something that had to be done, but no-one was going to thank you for doing it. The back door of the van was wide open and wonderful, warm, spicy smells were drifting out into the cold night air.

'Happy Birthday, Billy!' sang the twins.

'Thanks,' mumbled Billy, slightly embarrassed. 'Great smells!'

'Wait until you taste the things we've brought,' said Sandra. 'Mum and Dad have been in the kitchen since six o'clock this morning. There's wind-dried duck, Peking duck, dumplings, noodles, pancakes, spring rolls . . . everything!'

'Any bird's nest soup?' asked Billy mischievously.

'*Yuk!* No! That stuff's disgusting,' retorted Sandra.

'Come on you lot, I need a hand,' said Mr Wong, handing me a metal tray piled high with warm, white dumplings.

'They're the Major's favourite,' said Sheila.

We ferried the feast across the lawn to the waiting tables, where Mam and Mrs Wong were lighting portable gas ovens to keep things hot.

'Look at this place!' exclaimed Sandra, gazing across the lawn towards the pond and the twinkling island. 'Everything's . . . perfect.'

'Yes,' I muttered glumly, looking to Billy for support.

'What's the matter?' asked Sheila. 'Has something happened?'

I took the letter out of my pocket and handed it to her. She studied it for a while the said, 'It's no big deal. It's a final demand. But you can pay a little bit each month.'

I turned Albert's electricity bill over and she read the letter.

'What does he mean, "that hotel in Monte Carlo"?'

'He means prison,' said Billy, flatly.

'*Prison!*'

'Why?' asked Sandra.

'The police found six stolen computers underneath his pumpkins.'

This seemed to take a while to sink in.

'Did *he* steal them?' asked Sheila.

'No, but he was hiding them. And maybe selling them. I don't know,' I said.

'What's going to happen to him?' asked Sandra quietly.

'It's happened,' said Billy. 'Six months in the clink.'

'Can I keep this?' asked Sheila, holding up Albert's letter.

'Yeah,' said Billy, shrugging his shoulders.

'Fine,' I added.

She folded it neatly and tucked it inside her black silk jacket. Then she walked off across the lawn. I was going to follow her, but Sandra grabbed my arm.

'Leave her,' she said softly.

By half past seven the cars were bumper to bumper and the lawn was milling with people, laughing and chatting and carrying paper plates brimming with the delicacies being served by Mr and Mrs Wong and a few helpers. Dad had lit the bonfire and the sweet-and-sour smell of burning apple wood mingled pleasantly with the aroma of food. I was standing with Sheila and Sandra, watching the orange sparks dance upwards like a swarm of mad bees, feeling the heat from the flames, when Billy arrived back with his third helping.

'They're great these! Thisismeseventh,'

he mumbled, through a mouth full of dumpling.

'Can we give it to him now?' asked Sandra.

Sheila and I nodded and Sandra handed Billy a small parcel.

'What's this?' asked Billy.

'Open it and see.'

Billy put down his plate and opened the parcel. Inside there was a black leather collar covered in brass studs. The studs spelt 'NORMAN'.

'It's from the three of us,' said Sandra. 'For you *and* Norman. But we thought Norman might suit it better.'

'He'll love it!' said Billy. 'Thanks. This is the best birthday I've ever had.'

'*There* you are,' said Kit. 'I've been looking for you everywhere. How's the birthday boy?'

'Great. Have y'seen what they got me?'

'Very fashionable, I'm sure,' said Kit politely.

'It's for my dog.'

'Aaaah. Well, if we're giving presents, I've got a little something for the three of you. It's not much, more of a memento really.'

And she gave us each a small, round parcel loosely wrapped in white tissue paper. It was a lot heavier than I expected. We all pulled apart the tissue and gasped with surprise to see three glass eyeballs in each parcel staring upwards from the palms of our hands.

'Tigers' eyes,' said Kit. 'The same as I used for Boris.'

'Thanks! They're brilliant.'

'Thank *you*,' she said.

And left as Sam Warner arrived.

'Have y'tried these dumpling things? I don't know what they've got in them, but they're amazin'. What're you lot eating?'

'Tigers' eyeballs,' said Sheila, holding out her arm and opening her hand.

'I didn't see them. It's *my* birthday soon. My dad says, if I want to, we can go to the Red Dragon. Is that all right?'

'Yes, Sam,' laughed Sheila. 'Of course it's all right.'

The moon had risen from behind the wood and was climbing into the sky. Over by the house a bell rang. The laughing and chattering dwindled away and everyone turned to Major Gregory who was standing by the front door with Mr and Mrs Wong seated on his left, and Gran seated on his right. Gran looked amazing. She'd put her hair up in a bun the way Chinese ladies do with black and gold lacquered sticks poking through to keep it in place. Round her neck was a little pearl necklace that I hadn't seen before and her eyes were twinkling in the candlelight.

'Ladies and gentleman, boys and girls,' began

the Major. 'Welcome to the Mid-Autumn Festival at the Old Manor. For those of you who are not already aware, this is a traditional Chinese festival celebrating the beauty of the moon. A moon much-loved by dragons. But this evening we have several other reasons to celebrate. We have no less than three birthdays – not all on this day, but near enough. Firstly we have that of the eternally youthful Mrs Florence Stoker.'

Gran looked up and gave him a friendly dig in the leg with her elbow.

Everyone laughed.

'Secondly, that of the now very grown-up Master William Gates.'

Lots of cheering.

'And last, and most definitely of least importance, my own.'

More cheers.

'I would also like to take this opportunity to thank the Red Dragon restaurant for the delicious banquet they have prepared for us this evening.'

Murmurs of agreement.

'And to welcome Mr and Mrs Wong and their charming daughters, Sandra and Sheila, to Larkstoke village. I am sure we all agree that their arrival in our midst has enriched our little community considerably.'

The applause eventually died away and the

Major placed his hand on Gran's shoulder. I thought his leg must be playing up.

'Finally,' he continued, 'I have a rather special announcement to make.'

He paused for a bit and all you could hear was the distant crackling of the bonfire.

'The engagement of Mrs Florence Stoker to Major Alexander James Alston . . .'

The place went mad. I couldn't believe what I was hearing. *Gran and the Major getting married?* I looked across at Mam, who was standing next to Mr and Mrs Wong, and I could see from the expression on her face that she was as gobsmacked as I was.

'Thank you! Thank you!' shouted the Major. 'And now, let the pyrotechnics begin!'

Everyone turned round as over by the apple trees Dad and Mr Warner lit the first of the fireworks, a giant rocket that *whooshed* up into the sky and exploded in a massive chrysanthemum of burning orange and pink. Then another, and another. Each one bigger and brighter than the last. Each one more spectacular, until it seemed like it was impossible to keep surprising people.

The last of the rockets exploded with a bang that seemed to shake the stones of the Manor. Brilliant purple balls of light filled the sky, hanging there like stars, for a few magic seconds, then slowly tumbling into blackness. Everything went quiet. It seemed like it was all over. Then I saw Dad and Mr Warner crouching in front of the bamboo wall. There was a hissing noise and a trail of orange sparks began to crawl upwards from either end. They both ran for cover as the wall burst into a mass of sizzling colour. It was a tiger!

Everyone started shouting and cheering as it began shaking its head and 'roaring'. Its stripes were bands of orange sparks separated by the black of the night. Its teeth were brilliant white points of light surrounded by a cascade of crimson. And its eyes were green and gold balls of flame. It seemed angry and amazingly alive. Like it was desperately trying to leap from its frame and escape over the wall. Then gradually it seemed to lose its breath and, bit by bit, it fizzled out until all that remained were its burning eyes.

'We should make a toast,' suggested Sandra, raising her paper cup.

'I'm stuffed,' said Billy. 'I couldn't eat another thing.'

'A toast to the happy couple,' she said exasperatedly.

We all raised our cups.

'The happy couple,' I said, still stunned.

Sheila jerked her head and tossed back her ponytail.

'There's one other toast we should make,' she added.

'What's that?' I asked.

'To absent dragons,' she said, staring solemnly at the moon.

'To Albert,' I said.

'*One for all!*' shouted Billy.

'*And all for one!*'

Forgotten in the darkness, the firework tiger gave a final splutter and closed his eyes.

THE END